LIFE BLOOD

Cora's Choice – Book 1

V. M. BLACK

Aethereal Bonds
aetherealbonds.com

Swift River Media Group
Washington, D.C.

ISBN: 1496062515
ISBN-13: 978-1496062512

FICTION / General
FICTION / Coming of Age
FICTION / Fantasy / Urban
FICTION / Gothic
FICTION / Political
FICTION / Romance / General
FICTION / Romance / New Adult
FICTION / Romance / Paranormal
FICTION / Thrillers / Supernatural
FICTION / Thrillers / Political

In The Vampire's Office

SHADOWS CROWDED IN THE CORNERS of Mr. Thorne's office, spilling toward the center of the room. The marble tile of the rest of the office gave way to elegant parquet here, scattered with rugs that were worth every penny of my student loans and more.

"Ah, Ms. Shaw." The voice came from the shadows at the far end of the room. It was rich, low, and dark with some private humor.

I stepped forward, feeling the heat rise in my cheeks. "Cora," I offered.

"Yes, I know. Please, take a seat. I have your medical record here, Ms. Shaw," the man continued. Hands emerged from the shadow—strong and masculine, with long blunt fingers. He flipped open the laptop in front of him with a carelessly graceful gesture.

"Cora Ann Shaw. T-cell prolymphocytic leukemia. Terminal. Is that correct?"

The cold summary hit me like a blow.

"Yes," I managed. "That's right. Dr. Robeson said you could help me."

He leaned forward into the light of his laptop screen, and I caught my breath.

"Perhaps. Perhaps I can."

Aethereal Bonds

aetherealbonds.com

Cora's Choice

Life Blood
Blood Born
Bad Blood
Blood Rites
Blood Bond
Blood Price

The Alpha's Captive

Taken
Pursuit
Flight
Haven
Escape
Freed

ACKNOWLEDGEMENTS

Special thanks to my ever-patient family.

CONTENTS

CHAPTER ONE

"No response," I repeated, staring numbly at the upside-down chart on the doctor's desk. "None."

"I am sorry," Dr. Robeson said. "There is really no point in keeping you on the alemtuzumab any longer."

"But you said that it's the only thing that could help," I protested. "It has to work."

"Cora, I have your latest lab results right here." She tapped the open folder. "Your lymphocytes are continuing to climb. Right now, the only thing the alemtuzumab is doing is decreasing your quality of life."

I could see my name at the top of the chart: Cora Ann Shaw. There I was, summed up in black and white. My height—a little less than average. My date of birth.

My weight, which had fallen from I'd-like-to-lose-10-pounds to terrifying double digits. And, of course, my diagnosis: T-cell prolymphocytic leukemia.

Cancer. To me, it had meant pink ribbons, surgical scars, and middle-aged women without hair. I hadn't even heard of T-cell leukemia then. I hadn't realized how the cancer could steal all my strength, burn through my fat and then consume even my muscle to feed itself as I wasted away.

"There must be other things to try," I pushed. "Some other chemotherapy."

"I'm very sorry," the oncologist said again. "The older therapies were ineffective. That's why their use has been discontinued. They simply don't prolong life—in fact, on average, they shortened it. Alemtuzumab was our only realistic shot."

I should get a second opinion, I thought. Except Dr. Robeson was my second opinion. *I'm at Johns Hopkins, for godssake,* I thought bleakly. *Where else can I go?*

"So," I said. "Five months, then."

"It could be that long," Dr. Robeson said carefully.

I felt the tears burning my eyes, and I blinked them away. "You promised me seven months. That wasn't even two months ago."

Dr. Robeson had a bulletin board on her office wall. It was full of the happy pictures and notes from those she'd cured and even a few grateful letters from those she hadn't. Mine wasn't going to go there. I wouldn't know what to say. *Thanks for trying* didn't seem quite generous enough. Anything more would have been fake.

"Cora, cancer has a different rate of progression for everyone—"

"I know," I said, cutting her off. I was being unfair. I knew it, and it made me squirm inside.

But I don't want to be fair. Damn it, I just want to live!

"I'm turning twenty-two in two months," I continued. "I'm graduating—*supposed* to be graduating—from the University of Maryland in six months. I've applied to grad school."

"I know, Cora." And there was genuine sympathy there, behind the professional wall that kept her insulated from all the people she couldn't save.

I took a deep breath and pushed to my feet. My hips hurt from the institutional chair, my buttocks too thin now to cushion them. "Sorry. I was just hoping for better news."

"So was I." Dr. Robeson opened a drawer and pulled out a brochure. "This is an excellent hospice program. Your student insurance will cover all the costs beyond the deductible, and there are many people there who will be happy to help you."

It took all my will to force myself to accept the shiny trifold of cardstock from her. I squeezed it a little too hard, and it creased in my hand. "Thank you," I heard myself say.

"I can, of course, continue to treat you, addressing symptoms as they arise, infections and the like, making sure you're as comfortable and healthy as possible for as long as possible. I'm happy to do so. But I can't slow the progress of your leukemia." The oncologist hesitated. "There is one other possibility. A chance in thousands. If it works...." She cocked her head sideways as if she were gauging me, then gave a shrug so small I almost missed it. "Anyway, here's his card. You can hear him out, at least. Decide for yourself if the risk is worth it."

She extended a small, linen-colored business card with a discreet black border. On it was a phone number. No name, no details, just a simple copperplate number inscribed in the center of the card.

"Thank you," I repeated, blinking at it.

"I've already filled out the referral," Dr. Robeson said. "All you need is to give hospice a call, if that's what you decide. Or the other number—he's expecting your call, too."

"Yeah," I said. I swallowed. "Goodbye."

"Bye. Enjoy your Christmas," the doctor said with reflexive pleasantry.

"Yeah," I said again. I shoved the brochure and the card in my jacket pocket and stumbled from the office.

The carpeted halls of the professional wing were dotted with brisk nurses in scrubs and plastic clogs. I hated them all. Blinking hard, I willed them not to look at me and measured the distance from the oncology department to the nearest exit in my mind.

Keep it together for just a few seconds more, Cora. You're almost there.

Head down, I blew past the bank of elevators and burst through the heavy fire door into the stairwell, forcing my tired legs to keep up as I flung myself down the stairs to the ground floor.

At the bottom, I ducked out the side door and into the cold. I found myself in a small, semi-concealed alcove between two wings of the building. No one could see me, at least for the moment. I let my legs give out, sinking to the sidewalk with my back against the institutional brick, half-gasping and half-sobbing.

Five months. Or less.

It wasn't fair!

Finals were next month. I'd already picked out my classes for the next semester. Sent in my tuition.

I wondered if I should withdraw. But why bother? It wasn't like I'd live long enough even to owe payments on my student loans.

Enjoy your Christmas. The last Christmas I'd enjoyed had been two years ago, before Gramma died. Now there was no one left. I'd gone home with my roommate Lisette and her sister the last year, but I'd been miserable with missing my Gramma and even more miserable trying to pretend that everything was fine. I didn't think I had the strength to try to smile through the season again with the specter of my death hanging over the festivities. I'd already decided that it would be better for everyone if I stayed in our university apartment alone.

I dashed away the betraying tears and got my phone out of my pocket. Lisette would want to know the news. My finger hovered over her name on the screen. She deserved to be told. When she'd found me crying in my room the day I got my diagnosis, she'd given me one of her huge hugs and said I was going to beat the cancer, and she was going to be there for me until I did.

She'd held up her end of the bargain. I couldn't tell her that I wasn't going to hold up mine.

I pulled the brochure out and smoothed it. There was a photograph, the edges artfully out of focus, of an elderly woman being hugged by a smiling model who could have been any age from thirty to fifty-five. The text was full of words like "care," "comfort," and "dignity." The toll-free number stared at me, but I couldn't make myself call it, either.

There was the other paper—the card, rather, small and mysterious, with the single phone number on it. The cold from the hard cement under me was beginning to seep into my bones, and the wind chilled my wet cheeks. I shifted. What did I have to lose?

I entered the number and looked at it for a long moment before I touched the send button. The phone rang once as it connected, then once again.

"Name?" The voice was male, light and impersonal.

Taken aback, it took me a moment to respond. "Cora Shaw."

"Please proceed to the emergent care entrance, Ms. Shaw," the man said. "A car will meet you there. Thank you."

"But—" I said. I looked at the phone. The time was flashing on the display—he had already hung up.

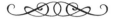

Chapter Two

O kay. Weird.

I thought about redialing, but I didn't really see the point, except maybe to complain about him hanging up on me—which, on reflection, seemed like a pretty stupid thing to do.

Well, then. *The emergent care entrance*, he'd said.

I pushed to my feet and looked around. The medical center I'd just left squatted in the center of the Johns Hopkins Bayview campus, a flat expanse of frost-browned lawn stretching around it to the distant street. There were other buildings scattered across the vast campus, but I figured the emergency department had to be somewhere in the main center. Where, though, I couldn't guess.

I could go back inside. There would be signs and directories there. But there were also too many people, too many bustling nurses and bewildered visitors. I'd just escaped the hospital. I couldn't make myself go back.

I zipped up my jacket and flipped up the hood. I hadn't bothered to take it off inside the offices. I was always cold now, even inside. I picked a direction and began walking around the brick and glass monstrosity of the main hospital building.

A car will meet me? How strange was that?

I don't have to go, I told myself. But I needed to do something. Something other than just wait to die.

The wind grew suddenly sharper as I got farther from the building along the main sidewalk that circled it. I shoved my hands in my pockets. Fatigue dragged at me with every step. I would pay tomorrow for this walk—never mind the blind flight down the stairs.

I turned the first corner of the building. There was no sign of a drive or a big entrance, only the long blank façade continuing uninterrupted for hundreds of feet.

Crap. With my luck today, the emergency department would be all the way on the third side, and I'd chosen the long way around.

Would I make it? And if I didn't, how long would it take for someone to find me?

I shoved those thoughts down.

By the time I rounded the second corner of the medical center, I was winded and my legs were shaking. My heart clenched with relief at the sight of the circular drive and the wide canopy jutting out from the building over it.

Emergency, the sign spelled out above it. I trudged on, shutting out pain and exhaustion as I fixed my eyes on that word.

I stumbled under the protection of the canopy at the hospital entrance and leaned against one of the big square columns, taking some of my weight off my trembling legs and struggling to catch my breath.

"Ms. Shaw?"

I pushed aside my exhaustion and looked up. There, at the curb, stood a man in an old-fashioned chauffeur's uniform, complete with hat and gloves. The car he stood next to was an understated silver color, but the elegant shape screamed money. A Bentley, I realized as I recognized the symbol on the trunk.

Oh, really?

"I'm Cora Shaw," I said cautiously.

The driver opened the rear passenger door. "Please, enter."

I gaped at him for several seconds. I mean, a Bentley? I didn't know what I had expected, but it wasn't this. Maybe a yellow cab. The man on the phone had told me that they would send a car. And here it was. But that didn't make it seem any less bizarre. It was, I decided, more than a little creepy.

"How do I know you're not trying to kidnap me?" I demanded, crossing my arms across my chest.

"I must admit, Ms. Shaw, that this is often a fear of our patients," the chauffeur said evenly.

I waited for him to continue with his reassurances, but he simply stood, waiting impassively.

I shifted against the cold column. I could see the soft interior from here, and my whole body clamored for a chance to settle into the warm comfort it offered.

What if he was a kidnapper? I wondered. What was the worst that could happen? Well, I could get brutally mutilated and murdered, I supposed. Torture would be bad, but my death was coming pretty soon, anyway.

On the other hand, the best that could happen was, of course, a cure. I barely let myself think that for the tiniest instant before shutting it away. I'd already had my hopes dashed today. I didn't need to create new ones only to have them destroyed, too.

I looked at the car and its driver again. He didn't *seem* like a serial killer. And as weird as this all was, the number I'd called had come from my doctor.

Still....

Oh, to hell with it. I sent a quick text to Lisette: The last # I called was 202-324-6475 n they sent driver to hospital to pick me up. Will txt or call in 2 hrs.

Then I turned off the ringer and alerts even as Lisette's first text arrived, shoved the phone in my pocket, took a deep breath, and got into the car.

The chauffeur closed the door as I struggled out of my jacket. The interior was all fawn leather and burled wood, with two wide seats contoured into the back bench. A dark screen was mounted into the headrest in front of me. I shoved my coat down at my feet and sat back, and the warmth of the heated seat crept into my aching bones as it cradled my body. I hadn't realized how much I hurt until it was soothed away.

The chauffeur got into the driver's seat, and the

snap of his car door closing brought me back to myself. With a sudden pinch of guilt at holding him up, I buckled hurriedly.

"Where are we going?" I asked.

"Mr. Thorne is here in Baltimore today," he said, shifting into drive. "The office is not far."

The leather molded itself to every muscle, and I surrendered to its embrace, letting exhaustion settle over me like a thick blanket. It was easiest to sink into the warmth and let my fears go to sleep as the buildings passed by the tinted windows in a blur.

I roused myself from my daze as we passed the Inner Harbor. The car swung up one of the side streets, and in a moment, the driver pulled up to the curb and sprang out, swinging open my door before I had time to do more than unbuckle and gather my jacket.

"Top floor, Ms. Shaw," he said, giving me a fractional bow.

A bow? Really?

"Thank you," I managed awkwardly.

The old building towered from the sidewalk in front of me, half columns of white marble flanking the high arched windows before defaulting to red brick above. The great stone letters on the frieze were darkened with the grime of a century: FIRST BANK OF BALTIMORE. But there had been no such bank in my lifetime, and there was no indication of what the building was used for now.

It didn't look much like a clinic or a biotech company, but it had to be one of them. What else could help me now?

I climbed the six steps up to the brass double doors, taking note of the address in gold letters on the glass of the transom above. Linen shades shrouded the glass. The right door yielded reluctantly to my pull, and I stepped inside.

I found myself in a marble lobby, accented with brass pots and burnished mahogany. Each of the great windows had a shade drawn over it, shutting out the street, cutting the building off from the world. Elegant people dressed in sharp suits strode across the room and spoke in low, urgent tones in corners among the groves of potted ficus. None of them spared me a glance. Among pencil skirts and neat ties, my sweater and jeans were definitely out of place.

I'd had an internship with the corporate arm of an insurance company the summer before, and it had been nothing like this. This was the kind of scene that you saw in a movie—not a real office but the Hollywood image of one, where everyone was just a little too attractive, just a little too put together, and everything was just a little too polished.

My stomach twisted with sudden uncertainty. What was this place? Where were the other patients, the nurses, the waiting room?

The receptionist across from the doors took note of me and raised her eyebrows. "May I help you?"

"Cora Shaw to see...Mr. Thorne?" I asked weakly. I hoped I remembered the name right.

The woman smiled briefly, nodding at the central elevator. "He's waiting for you, Ms. Shaw. Go on up. Penthouse office."

I went to the elevator, the shaft of which was wrapped in the curve of the staircase. It opened as soon as I hit the button. A sign? I'd had such a catastrophically bad run of luck that I was ready for anything to be a sign right now.

I hit the twelfth floor, then fumbled in my jacket pocket for my cell, texting Lisette the full address of the building that I was in. She'd already blown up my phone with texts and calls, but I couldn't answer them. Not yet. Not when all I had to tell her was more bad news. But I was glad she'd already seen my message. Feeling safer, I shoved the phone back in my pocket as the doors opened.

Just like in the lobby, all the windows on this floor were shaded. A striking redhead sat behind the reception desk in an immaculate cream blouse and heavy pearls that I had no doubt were real. Again, I felt distinctly grubby and out of place, like a person who had wandered onto a stage set from off the street. I had dressed for class and a doctor's appointment, not this.

Whatever this was.

I had a sick feeling that there had been some confusion, some mix up. They wouldn't be able to help me at all. No one could....

"Ms. Shaw?" the woman asked, smiling with perfectly pitched pleasantry. "Mr. Thorne will see you now."

She must have pushed a button, because the tall mahogany doors beyond her desk swung open.

I braced myself and went inside. The doors closed silently behind me.

13

CHAPTER THREE

Shadows crowded in the corners of Mr. Thorne's office, spilling toward the center of the room. The marble tile of the rest of the office gave way to elegant parquet here, scattered with rugs that were worth every penny of my student loans and more. Oils of hunting scenes hung on the paneled walls, and the ceiling, at least a dozen feet above my head, was intricately coffered.

No, it didn't seem much like a biotech company at all.

"Ah, Ms. Shaw." The voice came from the shadows at the far end of the room. It was rich, low, and dark with some private humor.

I stepped forward, feeling the heat rise in my cheeks. "Cora," I offered.

"Yes, I know. Please, take a seat."

I could make out the shape of the man behind the enormous, gleaming desk, but the discreet lighting seemed designed to conceal his face. Two massive armless chairs crouched on lion's paw feet in the center of another thick rug. Cautiously, I took one, sitting on the very edge of the brocaded seat. The recessed light above me shone directly into my eyes. I squinted to see beyond it and could only get the impression of wide shoulders and dark hair.

"Mr. Thorne, I'm sorry. I think there must have been some kind of mistake," I began.

"There has been no mistake." That voice again—warm and amber. It was effortlessly intimate while being entirely polite.

I shivered slightly and wished that the door to the reception room was still open.

"I have your medical record here, Ms. Shaw," the man continued. Hands emerged from the shadows—strong and masculine, with long blunt fingers. He flipped open the laptop in front of him with a carelessly graceful gesture, and in the sudden glow, I could make out his features.

I swallowed hard. His black hair swept immaculately to the side, and his long jaw and broad forehead were balanced by an elegant, slightly aquiline nose. His face seemed a little too symmetrical, almost artificially so, like it belonged to the paintings on the walls instead of to a living, breathing man.

I wished suddenly that the lush rug under my feet could swallow me up.

"Cora Ann Shaw. T-cell prolymphocytic leukemia.

Terminal. Is that correct?"

The cold summary hit me like a blow. I opened my mouth, and for a moment nothing came out. He raised his gaze to meet mine. His eyes were icy blue, and they seemed to look right through me.

"Yes," I breathed. "That's right. Dr. Robeson said you could help me."

"You must understand that you are first required to pass the initial tests," he said, his brow low and stern.

"I understand," I said, even though I didn't.

Mr. Thorne opened a drawer and took out a small black case. He stood and circled the desk until he stood above me, so close that I might have reached out and touched the hem of his pinstripe suit jacket. He was, I thought, quite tall.

He set the case on the edge of the desk and unzipped it, opening it to reveal a kind of blood collection kit. I sat up straighter. With the last round of medication, I'd become used to regular injections, but I still wouldn't say that I was exactly blasé about needles.

And anyhow, blood collection? In an office? That was...unconventional.

"The results of the screening will indicate if you are a good candidate for the procedure," Mr. Thorne said. He selected a needle from the array inside the case, locking it into a holder. "But you must know, even if the outcome is encouraging, the treatment is only successful in a small minority of cases."

"How small?" I asked, as much to distract myself from his preparations as out of a desire to know the answer. I could always Google for details later.

"One in a hundred," he said. "Perhaps less."

"Oh," I said in a little voice. "That *is* small."

"And if the procedure is unsuccessful, it always results in death," he continued.

"Wait, what?" What the hell kind of procedure was that? "So a one percent chance of cure, and a ninety-nine percent chance of death? That doesn't sound like smart odds to me."

He looked up from the needle. His gaze pierced me, his eyes deep and hollow under his straight black brows. As handsome as he was, he didn't exactly look the picture of health, either. "What are your chances now?"

I opened my mouth, then shut it. My chances were exactly nil. Put that way, gambling on an outside chance didn't seem quite so insane.

"That is why we only select terminal patients," he said, pulling out a glass blood collection tube.

"What about relapse?" I demanded. As a cancer patient, I'd learned that the disease could lurk in my body for months or years, undetectable until it spread out again to kill me.

"There is no risk of relapse. If you are cured, you are cured." That mesmerizing gaze caught me again. "Forever."

He dropped to one knee next to my chair, and my heart did an unexpected backflip. Oh, God, he was a beautiful man, more beautiful than he had any right to be. I tried to think about something else, anything else, because this certainly wasn't the right kind of response of a patient to her doctor. But this close, I could smell his cologne, all sandalwood, leather, and musk, and my mind refused to obey my order to find something else to dwell on. *Pink elephants, pink elephants, pink elephants....*

How old was he? I wondered. He carried the authority of an older man, but this close, I could see that his pale skin was almost inhumanly flawless, not so much young as...perfect.

Damn. At least it was too dark for him to see my furious blush.

He held out a hand. I stared at it for a moment before I realized that he wanted my arm.

"Shouldn't you be wearing gloves?" I asked.

"I am not at risk of blood contamination," he said, sounding unaccountably amused.

For some reason, I believed him, even though I had no reason to. I gave him my arm, inner wrist facing upwards. His fingers touched my skin, cool and commanding, as he slid the sleeve of my sweater up to bare the crease of my elbow. It sent a deep shiver through me, a tightening in my center that made me blush even harder. My jacket slipped from my lap to crumple on the floor between us. I tried not to look at him, but I could not stop myself from staring at the top of his head with such intensity that I was half-surprised that his impeccably combed hair didn't combust.

He's about to stick you with a needle, you idiot, I snarled at myself. *Don't you have any sense or dignity at all?*

He looked up at me, one side of that delicious mouth quirking, and my breath tangled in my lungs. *No, no I don't,* I thought distantly. *No sense or dignity at all.*

Mr. Thorne wiped the inside of my elbow with an alcohol-soaked swab. The smell of evaporating ethanol turned my stomach a little.

"It won't hurt," he said, discarding the swab and taking up the needle. "I promise."

I started to protest such an absurd claim, but just then, the needle met the skin above my vein. Something else happened at the same moment—some sensation that came from the touch of his hand against my wrist. It spiraled outward, up my arm and deep into my center, rippling back up into my head so suddenly that I gasped. The needle pushed through my skin at the same moment that a heady wave welled up to carry the pain of the needle and turn it into a deep, twisting sensation that sent my heart racing as heat flooded my groin.

I stared at the needle in my arm as the shivering reaction swept over me. My skin was burning, my body flushed against the impossible coolness of his fingers. The blood collection tube was almost full. Swiftly, Mr. Thorne pulled it free, then slipped the needle from my vein.

"No—" I said involuntarily as the sensation was cut off. I needed—I needed it back. I needed *him*.

What was wrong with me?

I turned my bewildered gaze to Mr. Thorne. His face was still as pale as ivory, but there was a dark glitter in his hooded eyes that matched my need and sent my heart glittering out of control.

"What did you do to me?" I whispered.

"You would say yes," he said, the dark hunger of his voice tinged with an infinite sadness as he stood and discarded the used needle, setting the blood collection tube upon the desk. "If I told you right now that I knew you would die, you would still say yes."

"I don't know what you're talking about," I said, even as my body said, *I would—to anything, anything at all...*

He bent over me, and I tried not to notice the scent of him. He touched the bead of blood that had formed upon the needle's exit. I could hear his breathing now—irregular as mine had become. With the tip of his forefinger, he scooped up the droplet, holding it suspended just as he held me with the force of his regard.

A shudder went through his frame, and he curled his fingers into a fist, smearing the blood across his palm. Suddenly, he seemed to grow, as if some darkness were uncurling inside him, extending past the limits of flesh and bone.

"Go," he ground out. "Go now, before I damn my best intentions."

It was as if some invisible bonds that had been holding me to my chair had been broken. I sprang up, snatched up my jacket, and fled, banging through the tall mahogany doors and not stopping until I jabbed the down button on the elevator.

"Goodbye, Miss Shaw," the secretary said unconcernedly from behind her desk. "You can expect the results within a week."

The door slid open, and I stumbled into the elevator compartment, slapping at the ground floor button frantically until the doors finally, reluctantly, closed.

CHAPTER FOUR

The elevator began to move, and I let out a breath of air I hadn't realized I'd been holding.

What the hell had just happened?

That man—Mr. Thorne—clearly he's some kind of perv. He's dosed me, roofied me or something.

How? I asked myself. With the power of his hands? Oh, God, that was what it had felt like. I lifted my hands to my cheeks. Even now they were flushed. And he had felt it, too. I knew what desire looked like, and that impossibly handsome man had desired...*me.*

It wasn't that I thought I was unattractive. But I'd come there as a patient seeking medical advice. What was his game? What did he want, other than patients for his trial? And why?

I stepped from the elevator back into the lobby. The receptionist looked up and greeted me with another bright smile, a jarring counterpoint to the man who lurked in darkness in the office above. "The car is waiting for you, Ms. Shaw. You will be taken back to your vehicle."

I nodded to her and went outside. The Bentley hummed at the curb, and the chauffeur opened the door at my approach. Dumbly, I sat inside, and the car rolled away.

My body ached, but it ached with a far different kind of pain than that which had become my constant companion in the last few months. It was a part of me that I had thought had died, stolen by the sickness months ago. Now all my nerves were awake and singing, and I had nothing to tell them because they only wanted one thing.

Him.

I hardly noticed when the chauffeur pulled up behind my battered Ford Focus in the parking garage. I didn't even think to ask him how he knew where I was parked or what my car looked like. I was far beyond wondering about those kinds of things.

I ducked out of the car, fumbling for my keys as I stepped unsteadily onto the concrete. By the time I had opened the driver's side door of my Focus, the Bentley had purred out of sight. I collapsed into the chill of the driver's seat. I wondered if I had just imagined everything. Already, it seemed as insubstantial as the clouds that materialized with my every breath, evaporating before I drew the next. I pushed up my sleeve and stared at the tiny needle prick there. I shivered as a shadow of sensation went through me again.

I closed my eyes, leaning my head against the edge

of the steering wheel. My phone dug into my stomach, which reminded me—*Lisette.*

Abruptly, I opened my eyes and started the engine, the car coughing to life in the cold.

What the hell was I going to tell Lisette?

At the door of our campus apartment, I stopped and tried to rub some color into my cheeks, dredging up my last reserves of strength before I went in. Lisette was already worried sick about me, and I didn't have much good news to give her. She didn't deserve to be burdened more.

I unlocked the door and pushed it open in the same movement.

"I'm back!" I called as I headed down the short hall to the living area.

Lisette looked up instantly from her laptop. "Hey, Cora's here," she said to the faces on the screen. "Gotta go."

"Hi, Cora!" the faces chorused, waving with forced cheer. "Bye, Cora!" Hannah and Sarah hung up.

Lisette opened her mouth—to scold me for my strange texts, no doubt—but taking a look at my face, she seemed to change her mind and treated me to a brittle smile instead.

I never was very good at fooling her.

"I grabbed some extra dinner for you at the dining hall," she said, patting the foam takeout box. "Eat. Chelsea and Christina are already gone."

For our senior year, Lisette, Chelsea, Christina, and I had ditched the dorms, which were dominated by underclassmen, for an on-campus pre-furnished apartment. There were four tiny bedrooms, two bathrooms, and a common kitchen and living area.

I felt a stab of guilt. Chelsea and Christina were probably already out drinking, but Lisette had put her own plans on hold to wait for me to come back.

"You don't have to stay in because of me," I said. "It's Friday. Sarah and Hannah will probably have a dozen people in their apartment by now."

"Maybe we'll go later." She shrugged and tossed her blonde hair over one shoulder. "So, what did the doctor say? Your texts didn't tell me anything."

I flopped onto the couch, kicking my feet up on the coffee table. I buried my chin in my jacket. "It didn't work."

"What?" Lisette's smile froze on her face.

"The alemtuzumab. It didn't work," I said. Saying it aloud seemed to make it more real. More hopeless. "The cancer's getting worse."

"Oh, Cora," Lisette said, her face crumpling. "What's she going to try now?"

I shook my head.

"Cora?"

Dammit. I blinked hard. I hadn't cried the whole trip from Baltimore to College Park. I wasn't about to start now. "She told me to call hospice."

"Hospice?" Lisette's voice rose. "But you're not—"

"Right," I said, cutting her off, not wanting to hear the word. "But she gave me another number. To a..." I hesitated, not sure how to describe it. "...a clinic."

That wasn't too much of a lie, was it? I wasn't quite able to explain the truth—I wasn't even sure what the truth was. I wanted to tell her more, but I didn't know what to say. Certainly nothing that would make her feel any better. Lisette saw black and white, right and wrong, and all I had for her were shadows. I tried to reach into the strangeness and pull out the facts.

I said, "They're working on a—a trial of sorts, I guess. The doctor drew some blood. They're going to run some tests, see if I'm a good candidate."

I realized I didn't have the name of the drug or the procedure. So much for Google.

"Gosh, I hope that you are!" Lisette said. She never swore.

"So do I." The significance of it all came crashing down on me all of a sudden, and I struggled to breathe against the weight in my chest. I wished that my Gramma was there. I wished I could put my head in her lap like I was a little kid again and have her pet my hair until I felt better.

But Gramma was gone, and it was selfish of me to want her here, to see me lose everything she'd worked so hard to give me as the cancer took it all away.

I took a deep, shuddering breath, and Lisette's face creased in deeper concern.

I stifled a groan. She deserved to deal with my illness even less than I did.

25

Lisette glanced at the door, then back at me. "You up for Hannah's place?"

I recognized the offer for what it was—a distraction—and I seized upon it.

"What's the plan for tonight?" I asked.

"They snagged Mike's Playstation again and have Netflix hooked up to the flat screen. Movie marathon. 1980s high school classics. Everybody's supposed to wear leg warmers and frizzy hair, but I think most of us are just going to show up in pajamas."

Hannah and Sarah lived in an apartment just down the hall. They threw a movie marathon at least once a month, and it always lasted well into the next day.

"What's showing?" I asked.

"*Ferris Bueller's Day Off, The Breakfast Club, Pretty in Pink, Risky Business.*"

I grinned. "Yeah, I think I'm up for that."

"Honestly?" Lisette lowered her voice in mock confidentiality. "I've only ever seen *The Breakfast Club.*"

"Me, too," I said.

"Finish your dinner, and then we can go and party like it's 1985," Lisette said.

I groaned and pulled the foam container over to myself, popping the lid.

"Philly cheesesteak. You like it," Lisette said encouragingly.

"I do, I do, and I swear I will eat every bite." I knew she'd stand over me until I did. I gave a half-shrug. "Well, now that I'm off the alemtuzumab, at least I'll be able to enjoy my food again."

"Maybe put some meat back on your bones." Lisette's voice was light, but she couldn't hide her worry.

"Sure thing," I said around the first bite of the only slightly soggy sandwich. "No problem."

An hour later, I sat in Hannah and Sarah's darkened living room, nibbling on a piece of pizza they'd bullied me into taking and leaning against a beanbag chair, wrapped in a hideous but surprisingly soft afghan that Sarah's grandmother had sent her.

And I felt normal again, if only for a little while.

Sarah was curled up in Mike's lap on one of the bland institutional chairs, not-quite-making-out and playing with the diamond ring on her finger. The rest of the girls and a couple of guys—boyfriends and wanna-bes—were sprawled around the room in various boneless poses.

I was suddenly, intensely glad that I was there and that I had them to be around me. If I'd stayed home that night, I would have probably cried and maybe puked and maybe cried some more. And at some point, Chelsea and Christina would have stumbled back in, probably drunk and almost certainly with at least one guy between them, and then I would have had to listen to them all night through the thin apartment walls.

It wasn't that I'd forgotten my grief. I was still dying, and I knew it. It was that, right now, I wasn't alone.

I dropped the greasy slice of pizza on the paper plate and let my eyes sag shut. For the moment, I was watching corny movies with my friends, and that was enough.

It was all I had.

CHAPTER FIVE

"So, remember—Spence says that school's primary value isn't to make you smart or even well-trained but to *signal* that you already have the qualities of intelligence that an employer is looking for," the professor said, summing up. "See you next week."

"So, basically, she's saying that what she teaches us doesn't really matter," said a guy two rows below me. His friend snorted.

I gathered my coat and shoved my notebook into my bag. I thought of the distance to my next class with a sick feeling in my stomach.

It was Thursday, six days since I had left Mr. Thorne's office bewildered and confused. Six days since the doctor told me that I had five months—*maybe* five months left to live.

I had tried very hard to keep all thoughts of that day out of my mind, and now that I didn't have to go in for an intravenous injection three times a week, I found that it was just possible to pretend, most of the time, that nothing was wrong.

Most of the time. As the one-week mark approached, though, I waited for news of the test with mounting anxiety. My last chance. As strange as the meeting with Mr. Thorne had been, and as much as I suspected a hidden agenda, I still believed he might be able to save me.

"Spence's job market signaling is only the first type that we will cover as applied to economics," the professor continued, raising her voice as we all clattered to our feet. "Next week, expect to cover the other applications discussed in Osborne, and don't forget to check the course site for the links to relevant online content. You will be responsible for *all* the material. Thank you!"

I slung my backpack over my shoulders, the weight dragging against me, just as my phone chimed, signaling that I'd missed a call during my preset no-ring for class. I pulled the phone out of my pocket and unlocked it. My heart skipped a beat when I saw the number.

It was the same one that I had dialed when I was first brought to Mr. Thorne.

I braced myself and stepped into the corridor, leaning back against the wall. Other students surged past me, laughing and joking about their plans for the weekend.

Setting my jaw, I hit the button to return the call. The phone connected, and again someone picked up on the first real ring.

"Ms. Shaw," the pleasant tenor said.

Not Mr. Thorne, but the same man who had answered the phone before.

"Yes?" My voice shook slightly, and I swallowed, trying to calm it. I closed my eyes, bracing myself for the final disappointment.

"Your lab results are in. Good news. You are an excellent candidate for the procedure."

"What?" I hit a high note that I hadn't intended. "I mean—I'm so...so pleased," I stuttered, still not certain that I had heard correctly.

After two months of bad news, to have something, even this small, seem to go right.... I half-considered pinching myself. Did people really do that?

The man on the phone continued coolly. "I can tell, Ms. Shaw. A car will be sent around to your apartment this evening. Six o'clock."

"I—I have to make the decision now?" I asked.

"No, Ms. Shaw. This is in the interest of full disclosure. Mr. Thorne will explain the procedure in detail, and you can decide how—and if—you wish to proceed."

If. A welter of emotions hit me at that word, and I remembered again the strangeness of our first meeting, the compulsion, the weird discord between what he presented to me and what he seemed to be. The light in his eyes, my blood a red smear across his hand.... I had kept all those thoughts clamped down, shut tight, because I had no choice. There could be no choice.

Not if I wanted to live.

"Okay," I said, ignoring the tightening in my center that I did not care to name. "I'll be ready, then. Six o'clock."

"Excellent. Goodbye, Ms. Shaw."

"Bye," I said, but the man was already gone.

I took a deep breath and let it out slowly. Six o'clock. A car would be waiting.

Okay, then.

"Can you explain to me again why you're wearing your interview skirt?" Lisette asked, frowning at me from the door to my bedroom. "And the blouse? To a doctor's appointment?"

"It isn't an appointment, exactly," I said. "More like a...consultation, or something."

"Isn't that like a British word for a doctor's appointment?" she said.

I adjusted the chignon at the back of my neck one more time. The one good thing about alemtuzumab was that unlike most chemotherapy, it didn't make your hair fall out. I still had the same ash brown waves that I'd always had, which, though not the most striking hair color, was a far sight better than being bald.

The bad thing about alemtuzumab, I thought, *is that it didn't work.*

"Look, the last time I showed up to a consultation

or appointment or whatever there, everybody was in business clothes." I dabbed concealer generously over the dark circles under my hollowed-out eyes.

"At a clinic," Lisette said flatly.

"I think the initial meetings are held at the corporate office," I said. "Anyway, if I'm going back there, I don't want to stick out again."

It was more than just being out of place. I had felt exposed in Mr. Thorne's office wearing my jeans and sweater. He had gotten under my skin, into my head. No one ever did that.

I wasn't dressing up for him. Not exactly. I was dressing up *against* him, hiding my sickness under cosmetics and fabric.

Hiding my weakness to him.

My Gramma used to break out her heels and her full palette of makeup whenever she had an important meeting at work or with the school. If it was really important, she wore the only suit she owned. She'd called it putting on her war paint.

"You don't have to look prettier or younger than they do," she used to say. "But if you look more put together, that's half the battle."

Well, I certainly wasn't going to look either more attractive or more put together than Mr. Thorne. But I hoped it would be enough.

"And that's the other thing," Lisette said. "The car. That's just weird."

"I think it's some kind of super-rich corporation. They really need volunteers for this drug trial." I swiped a light peach over my eyelids. It seemed to be successful in bringing some warmth back to my brown eyes.

"It's got to be crazy dangerous then," Lisette said.

Four quick brushes, and the mascara was on. Just my upper eyelashes—I looked tired enough already. "Probably. I'll find out tonight. But even trying something crazy dangerous is better than being declared terminal, which is all I've gotten so far."

"Well, you do look great," she said, almost begrudgingly.

"I feel like I'm playing dress-up." I rolled my eyes at myself. I'd had an internship in an office the last year, but I'd never really gotten used to the business clothes, and even there, I hadn't bothered with cosmetics beyond mascara and lip gloss.

I'm not really sure this is working for me, I thought, trying out the blush.

"Oh, God," I said. The rouge looked garish against my washed-out features. I reached for the washcloth.

"No, let me fix it," Lisette said. She grabbed a handful of toilet paper and dusted at my face. "Much better."

It was. "Thanks."

"Are you sure you've got enough energy for this?" Lisette fretted.

"God, Lisette, you're like the mother I never had. And never wanted," I said, but I smiled as I shook my head. "I napped for three hours this afternoon. I'm going to be fine."

"If you're sure," she grumbled.

I grabbed a safe peach lipstick and put it on. With my coral blouse, the cosmetics managed to bring some semblance of liveliness back into my face. Did I look stronger, too? I hoped so.

If I survived this, I decided, I would make a darned fine mortuary cosmetologist.

"Could I take your swing jacket?" I pleaded. "All I've got is my Columbia Sportswear coat, and it's not exactly businessy."

Lisette had been a couple of sizes larger than I was even before I got sick—with curves in all the right places, of course—but we could share coats and accessories. Not that there was much in my closet that she had an interest in, though she pretended otherwise.

"Sure thing," she said. "And you're taking a real purse?"

"Already put everything in it." I snatched her swing jacket from the sofa and grabbed my clutch and waggled it at her.

"You'd better head down now, then," Lisette said. "You're going to be late."

I paused at the door. "Don't wait up for me," I warned, knowing that she would, anyway.

She laughed. "Of course I will. Who else is going to get me through our game theory homework tonight?"

I smiled back at her, then hurried out the door.

The elevator down was crowded with other students I didn't know who eyed me curiously but didn't interrupt their conversations as they headed down. On the third floor, Geoff Nowak stepped in, all golden hair and bronze skin. He was in most of my classes—had been since freshman year.

"Hey, Shaw," he said, treating me to a dazzling

smile. He always called me Shaw because his stepmother's name was Cora, and he said it freaked him out to use the same name for me. "You look a bit dressed up for a date."

"It's more a business thing," I said, returning his smile.

"An interview?" The doors opened on the ground floor, and we all spilled out. "Who's interviewing now? If you're holding out on me...." He treated me to a patently fake threatening glare.

"Not an interview," I said as we went through the double doors. "Tell you later."

Like most of my friends, he didn't know I was sick. I wondered what exactly I'd tell him.

The Bentley was at the curb when we stepped out onto the sidewalk. The chauffeur swung the door open as I approached. Unable to resist, I gave Geoff a jaunty little wave before climbing in.

"Oh, snap," he called out after me, standing frozen on the sidewalk. "Shaw, you've got a lot to explain...."

The chauffeur shut the door and I settled back against the seat with my coat in my lap, feeling a little guilty. Geoff deserved a little teasing, but I had no idea what kind of excuse I was going to give him. Probably not a very good one, I thought.

"Where are you taking me?" I asked the driver, worried that I would be whisked away to Baltimore again. That would make for a long evening, even if the appointment was short, and I had class in the morning.

"Mr. Thorne has made arrangements in the District," the chauffeur said.

Vague but good enough, I supposed. I set my phone on silent and settled back against the seat to watch the lights of the city through the window, a yellow blur in the cold outside the car's heated cocoon, each block running into the next in an endless repetition of cement, asphalt, and brick.

I didn't realize that I had fallen asleep until the sound of my car door opening and the sudden breath of cold air roused me. I blinked a few times and surreptitiously wiped the drool from the corner of my mouth.

"We've arrived, Ms. Shaw," the chauffeur said helpfully.

"Where am I?" I ducked out of the car and stood on the sidewalk in front of a nondescript beige rowhouse, stretching my stiff muscles.

"The restaurant," the chauffeur said patiently. "Mr. Thorne is waiting for you."

I looked up, and I saw the sign: Komi. I swallowed. Even I had heard of Komi. One meal cost about the same as two weeks of dorm food. It was the current food mecca of the capital, impossible to score reservations unless you called at noon exactly one month ahead.

The chauffeur was already pulling away, so I had no choice but to mount the iron steps to the front door. I was desperately grateful that I'd decided to dress up. If I'd arrived in denim and sneakers, I would have died of humiliation right there and spared the cancer the trouble of killing me.

I swung open the door and stepped inside to be greeted by a black-clad host.

"You must be Ms. Shaw," he said, relieving me of my jacket. "This way, please."

I stepped forward after the host, my head still muddled with sleep and disbelief, not quite certain that I could trust any of this to be real. The narrow dining room was dim and intimate, with twelve tables that I counted as we passed.

There was a movement in the shadows of the farthest corner, and I raised my eyes as the host led me onward, knowing who it was even before I saw him—feeling him, somehow, in the darkness. And there he was, standing, watching me with his hungry eyes, wearing another impeccable three-piece suit and a black silk tie.

Mr. Thorne.

CHAPTER SIX

*H*e *really isn't* that *tall*, I thought as I took the chair the host pulled out for me. But that chiding did nothing to still the racing of my heart. Mr. Thorne looked down at me across the expanse of snowy linen. His slow smile was predatory.

Damn him, I thought, my breath catching. No one had any right to be that handsome. All my fussing in front of the mirror and whatever defense I thought I'd built with it went out the window with one look from him.

"I hope you understand that I cannot possibly afford this," I whispered tensely. "This is not exactly an insurable expense."

His lips quirked. I tried not to stare at them. "My treat."

I had the sense of undercurrents of meaning that I

didn't understand, of secret motives that went beyond my cure or even, for that matter, any kind of simple attraction to me. If Mr. Thorne wanted to seduce someone, he could do a far sight better than an emaciated, exhausted, dying college student.

I tried again. "I don't think this is the proper kind of setting for a doctor and patient to meet."

"Does the name *Mr.* Thorne mean nothing to you?" he asked, delicately stressing the title. "I am no one's doctor."

My stomach flipped over. Was this some kind of sick joke?

Before I could confront him, the sommelier appeared, bearing a bottle of wine. "You specified the Egon Müller Scharzhofberger Riesling Spätlese now and the Valdicava Brunello di Montalcino with the main course, sir?"

"Indeed," Mr. Thorne said.

The sommelier uncorked the white wine, pouring a small amount into the wineglass in front of him. Mr. Thorne sniffed it and nodded, and at his signal, the man half-filled first my glass and then his. I murmured my thanks reflexively even as my mind churned, waiting until she was out of earshot before I pounced.

"If you aren't a doctor, then what the hell do you think you are doing?" I demanded. "Why did you touch me?"

That wasn't what I had meant to say, and the words made my cheeks redden. *Way to keep the moral high ground, Cora.*

"Why did you take my blood?" I corrected. "Why

did you tell me you could help?"

He lifted the wineglass and took a small sip as if to hide his amusement. "One hardly needs a medical degree to be a competent phlebotomist. And I did not hear you protesting at my skill."

His fingers on my wrist... I could almost feel them again. I realized suddenly that my lips had parted, my breathing speeding up involuntarily.

I took a gulp of wine, angry and ashamed, and tried again. "If you're not a doctor, how can you help me?"

"Do you think I am playing at this?" His expression was grave.

"I don't know. How could I know?" The tears, never far from the surface now, pricked my eyes. I shoved them back mercilessly. "You seem rich enough to be able to play at anything."

"Not this," he said, his eyes narrowing. "Not with lives."

Not anymore.

That thought appeared abruptly in my head, as if it had been dropped there. Rattled, I looked away and tugged at my necklace, then took another—much more controlled—sip of my drink. I had a feeling that the bottle was ruinously expensive, full of subtleties and delicate bouquets that only the most refined palate could appreciate.

To me, it just tasted like white wine.

Another server materialized beside our table. "This evening's meal begins with a selection of twelve mezzethakia," he explained, setting a plate in front of each of us. "The first: smoked wild salmon with crème fraiche and coarse ground sea salt on a filigree of squid-ink toast."

The food looked exquisite, though it was small enough to finish in two bites.

"You ordered for me?" I asked as the server retreated back toward the kitchen, a little offended.

Again, that slow smile that melted my middle. "The menu is prix fixe," Mr. Thorne said.

I stared blankly.

He added, "It means you pay a great deal of money to eat whatever the chef cares to feed you." He lifted the salmon on toast in one piece, holding it as if he were saluting me. "Or, in this case, *I* pay a great deal of money."

He bit down, and I watched, mesmerized, at the movement of his teeth and lips. Another bite, and it was gone.

I blinked and looked down at my plate. There was something seriously wrong with me. No man could possibly be that fascinating. I picked up my own squid-ink toast, whatever that was. I took a hesitant bite.

Involuntarily I gasped, my gaze snapping up to meet Mr. Thorne's. The cream and salmon and salt melted together in my mouth, and the toast was the perfect level of crispness to balance the smooth melding of the other ingredients.

Mr. Thorne was watching me with half-lidded eyes. "Exactly," he said.

I ate it greedily—perhaps too greedily. It had been four days since my appetite had finally returned after discontinuing the alemtuzumab, and I couldn't have invented a better way to celebrate.

The rest of my protests died in my throat. Whatever reason he'd chosen to have our consultation at a restaurant, I was willing to go along for the ride, as long as that ride included more food like that.

As if by magic, our plates were whisked away as soon as I finished, and two more appeared. "A spoon of minced scallop with Greek yogurt dressing," the server explained before vanishing again.

It was a different taste revelation, complementary to the salmon toast but tart and complex.

"I didn't know that food could do this," I marveled. I considered whether it would be rude or—far worse—suggestive to put the whole bowl of the spoon in my mouth and suck off the last savory molecules of scallop.

"Think of all the other things in life you haven't had a chance to experience," Mr. Thorne said softly. "That you won't, unless you are cured."

Suddenly, I was no longer as hungry, and I set the spoon down. "And you believe that you can save me? You aren't even a doctor. Why should I trust you?"

He was doing that thing to me again, whatever it was, messing with my head. It was hard for me to confront him, to say the words that might mean the difference between life and death. I'd been my own health advocate since my first diagnosis. I'd read piles of studies, checked out mounds of medical books from the university library, even found Dr. Robeson because of her interest in T-cell leukemia. No man, however attractive, could push all that out of my brain.

But he could.

"I doubt the CEO of Merck has a medical license, either," he said. "Rest assured, I have a team of doctors at my disposal. Medical researchers, to be precise. And they have been working for years at making the outcome of our methods more reliable."

"So you do own a pharmaceutical company, then?" I asked as another course appeared before us. My Google searches for *Thorne* and *pharmaceuticals* had turned up nothing relevant.

"I own many companies. The medical research is but one endeavor, and it is not run for profit. In fact, none of the patients are charged for our services."

He took another sip of wine, and I found myself unconsciously starting to mirror him. With an effort, I put my hand in my lap instead. I needed to keep a clear head.

"So you do it out of the goodness of your heart, rescuing the terminal from their afflictions," I said, not bothering to keep the skepticism out of my voice.

"There is a benefit to me, as well," he said. "But you must fully understand the scope of the risk before you make a decision."

"Is that what this"—I waved my hand— "appointment or meeting or whatever is for?"

"Precisely."

"If you're supposed to be informing me of this procedure of yours, you're doing a bad job of it," I said. "All I seem to be doing is asking questions, and you're only half-answering them. If giving an explanation was what you wanted, we could have met in your office, like we did before."

His blue eyes went dark, and my breath caught. He held me in his gaze. "It is safer here."

"Safer," I echoed, somehow believing him even as I didn't understand.

"Look around you."

I did. Half a dozen servers bustled among twice as many tables in the warm candlelight.

"There are so many witnesses," he said, the words so soft I almost felt them more than heard them. "Too many witnesses to lose control."

I turned back to be caught up in his gaze again, knowing what he meant, the words calling up a shadow of the sensations that I had felt then to rush over me again. I saw my need reflected in his intensity, and I bit my lip hard. He felt it too, this connection between us. And that was far from reassuring.

"In my office, I nearly did something that I had sworn never to do again," he said.

"Attack me?" I said, my throat suddenly dry. The words came clumsily off my lips, and I knew they were wrong even as I said them. It hadn't felt like a potential attack, not then or in any of the thousand replays I'd tried to keep out of my mind.

Not even close.

His face tightened, though whether in anger or scorn, I couldn't tell. "I would do nothing to you—to anyone—that you wouldn't want me to. But it would still be wrong."

"How do you know what I'd want?" I whispered furiously, even as prickles of heat ran over my body to pool deep in my center. I shifted slightly in my chair, ignoring the tugging sensation between my thighs. "How dare you—*presume* to tell me what I want?"

I could have drowned in the darkness of his eyes. He reached across the table. I could not move. He took my chin in two fingers and rubbed his thumb along the line of my jaw. I leaned forward, into his hand, toward him. Every nerve sang in the wake of his cool touch, reaching so deep inside me that I whimpered, my hands curling into fists on the tabletop.

The corner of his lips lifted, and my heart stuttered. "You would have begged me."

I jumped when he released me just as the server set the next course in front of us. "Mascarpone stuffed date with olive oil and sea salt."

"Thank you," I murmured hoarsely. I did not lift my eyes from my plate until I had eaten it clean, embroiled in my sudden confusion and acute, excruciating awareness of the man across the table from me.

He was right. I knew he was right. I would have begged him—begged him for everything. But I didn't know why. What was wrong with me? Had I lost my mind?

And who was he, to do that to me?

I had to say something, to fill up the space between us with words, because what hung there now was too much for me to handle.

"Do you spend this much time with every patient?" I asked, pretending to busy myself with turning my wineglass to examine the glint of the wine in the candle-light.

"It depends on how far they make it through the process," he said evenly. "You must understand that nine out of ten are eliminated at screening. And of those who pass, a considerable number still decline the procedure."

I frowned at that, looking at my short fingernails rather than meeting that disconcerting gaze. "Are they all terminal? Like me?"

"Yes," he said. "Given the risks of the procedure, imminent death is a prerequisite."

I couldn't help myself then. I looked up to find him regarding me steadily. "Then why refuse it?"

"It is a choice of the last resort, Ms. Shaw," he said. "It comes with a ninety-nine percent chance of failure and death, as you noted so aptly last time we met. For many people, a certain death tomorrow is better than a near-certain death today."

"I don't think I'm going to die," I said. I didn't know where my conviction came from, but I was very sure.

"I want you to understand the gravity of your decision, Ms. Shaw. No one who makes this choice wants to die. Yet most still do. Once the procedure is begun, there is no stopping it. No turning back." The honeyed tone made the words almost soothing even though the meaning was blunt.

I shook my head. "Any chance is better than none." I stopped. "The procedure itself—is it so terrible? Is it an operation? Radiation? Chemotherapy?"

New plates were delivered, the old ones whisked away. I barely noticed the server's explanation of the

47

spanakopita.

"It is over in a matter of minutes," Mr. Thorne said. He twirled a fork in his fingers, and it glinted in the flame of the candle. "Blood is collected, and simultaneously, you are given an injection. The substance consists of a blend of long-chain molecules which function in some ways like a hemotoxin."

Toxin?

"That doesn't sound good," I said. That was probably the understatement of the year.

He set the fork down. "The hemotoxic effect is necessary to prepare for a fundamental and irrevocable reordering of the metabolism of every cell in your body. If your metabolism can change quickly enough in the wake of the hemotoxin, the cells are converted to a new state, and you live. If not, you die."

I set the spanakopita down untasted. "Haven't you tried to separate the components? So that the reordering or whatever happens without the hemotoxin?"

"Tried and failed," he said curtly. "For longer than you have been alive. The hemotoxic effect is a necessary precursor to the metabolic changes, and nothing we have attempted has been able to speed up the metabolic reordering. This current variation of our screening is the most successful breakthrough thus far."

"But one in a hundred," I objected.

His expression was severe. "One in one hundred who would otherwise die."

"So these metabolic changes...." I trailed off.

He raised an eyebrow. "They will revert your cancerous cells to a healthy state, all of them, swiftly and permanently. The extraneous cells should undergo an accelerated senescence and healthy function should return to the remaining ones immediately."

I thought about that for a moment, turning it over in my mind. Senescence. That meant aging.

"It is a cure, then," I said slowly. "A real cure. Not a remission. Like you said before, the cancer can't come back."

As I was trying to absorb that, another server appeared, bearing two platters, one with steaming meat, the other with various artful additions. "The entrée," she said, setting it between us. "Spit-roasted young goat with pita and the chef's culinary embellishments."

Mr. Thorne gave her a wave of thanks as she discreetly retired. I ignored the entrée.

"Not a remission," he agreed. "It is a cure for your present condition and as good as an immunization against any future cancer."

"How is that possible?"

His smile was rueful. I could hardly tear my gaze from his lips. "We don't know that, either. The mechanism is, of yet, very poorly understood."

One in one hundred. Well, I seemed to be good with long odds—my chance of developing the type of leukemia I had was one in tens of thousands, my chance for the alemtuzumab proving ineffective one in ten of that. Put that way, as illogical as it was, one in one hundred seemed like almost a sure thing.

Could I even trust myself around him? My judgment? I knew he had a very unscientific interest in me. Maybe he was just some kind of rich sadist who liked to

49

get into dying girls' heads and muck with them, make them hope for things that weren't real.

But if it was a chance, and Dr. Robeson believed it was, what choice did I have?

"I want it," I said, almost before I knew I had made the decision. "I want to live. If it's my only chance—"

"I will not take your answer now." Mr. Thorne cut me off. "You must think about it. Call in two weeks."

"Why?" I demanded. "I don't want to wait. I've made my decision. I'm ready to roll the dice now."

His hooded eyes burned with intensity. His eyes and cheeks were even more hollow now, I noticed, but they simply put a hard edge on his handsomeness. "Because I want you to say yes too badly. And sitting across from me, you will refuse me nothing that I want."

His words went through me even as I denied them. "Don't be ridiculous."

"Do you not believe me?"

The force of his attention had me pinned in my seat. My breath caught. I opened my mouth to disagree, but nothing came out. Still, I managed to shake my head.

"Put your hand in the candle, Ms. Shaw."

CHAPTER SEVEN

hat? My lips formed the word, but he had stolen the breath from my lungs. His gaze grew sharper, and I felt him, somehow, felt him through the shiver of my body, hot and cold. My hand rose. I tried to stop it, to tell it no, but I wanted this. I wanted it so badly that my bones ached.

My breath came more quickly with a fluttering deep inside that had nothing at all to do with nervousness. I could almost feel his hands on me again, could feel my body tuning to his. My body prickled with heady anticipation, not the fear of harm but the expectation of pleasure.

I reached for the candle that sat between us. A soft sound escaped my lips, and even I didn't know what it meant. I extended one finger, thrusting it into the flame. The fire danced around my fingertip, sending the most exquisite pain up through my arm until I gasped with it, welcoming it, meeting with a wrenching sensation deep in my core that was a very different kind of heat.

In an instant, it was gone. I blinked, panting. The flame was extinguished—his hand, cool and strong, was over my hand, my finger immersed in his water glass. Through the dripping sides of the water goblet, I could see the border of angry red flesh with a white blister in the center.

I watched, stunned, as he lifted my hand from the glass to his mouth. Keeping my gaze with his icy blue eyes, he bent his head until his lips met my blistered finger, sucking the drops of water from it.

My voice was not mine—it moaned, softly. A shudder went through my body, pure pleasure as my heated senses screamed at the touch. I pushed back against my chair without meaning to, my feet bracing against the ground.

He dropped my hand, and I was left reeling, gasping, my finger throbbing to the hammering of my heart.

"What are you doing to me?" The words were half-question, half-plea.

"Nothing but what is in my nature." His expression was full of regret—and hunger.

"I can't—" I stopped. "You can't—"

I stared at my finger. The blister was every bit as real as the flame had been.

"It's not possible. I wouldn't do that," I said, even as I remembered the ecstasy of pain. "I never would."

"But you did," he said.

I did. I did. I remembered it, I felt it, I had wanted it.... The pain and the pleasure all tangling into a mass of sensation so intense that it was like drinking pure life. If he told me to do it again, I would.

Maybe I was going mad. Maybe he was driving me mad.

"What are you?" I demanded.

"Something more dangerous than you can imagine," he said, and I believed him. Oh, how I believed him.

"What you are promising me—the cure. Is it real?" *Or do I also believe that because you want me to?*

His voice was fervent, his brows lowering. "Oh, it is very, very real, Cora Shaw. I have no need to lie to you to take what you would freely give."

He was right. I knew he was. I closed my eyes, but I could still see him in my mind, looking at me, looking through me. He could hurt me. The throbbing of my finger had reached my wrist now, a very real pain. He had hurt me. But still I wanted to give him everything.

"That is why you must decide for yourself," he said gently. "Far away from here. Far away from my influence, and far away from me."

Though only anticipated, I already felt the separation like a jolt. "No," I breathed, my eyelids flying open.

The sorrow on his face wrung my heart even though I didn't understand it. "You may be the one, after all, Ms. Shaw. But I will have your permission, of your own free will. Not now."

"In two weeks," I said then, defeated.

"In two weeks," he agreed. "Not a day before. You have the number."

I nodded dumbly.

"Then call. And if you still wish to gamble the last months of your life on an outside chance, I will be happy to assist you." He treated me to a lopsided smile that made my lungs hurt. "For now, you have a dinner to enjoy in the finest restaurant that a glittering capital can boast. Enjoy."

The rest of the evening was a long blur, my unrelenting awareness of him pushing all my senses to a fever pitch. Even the food became a kind of torture, the delight of my taste buds only throwing my frustration into contrast. After the entrée, which was a balance of perfected simplicity and intricate garnishes, came a series of tiny desserts, each more decadent than the last, spaced to titillate and to indulge. Every taste was enmeshed with the overwhelming force of Mr. Thorne's presence, every bite taken with keen knowledge of his closeness and of his gaze upon me.

At the end of the meal, I fled to the ladies' room with equal parts relief and longing. As I washed my hands, I stared at my own reflection, trying to find the Cora I knew within it. Strands of my hair were escaping to curl around the sides of my face, and my cheeks had the first real flush that I'd seen in months. The shining dark eyes I barely recognized. They couldn't be my own, because I saw depths in them that I didn't understand.

I squared my shoulders, scooped up my purse, and pushed back into the dining room. Mr. Thorne stood as I approached. Despite my attempts at control, I could hear my heart in my ears as he stepped forward to meet me.

"I've settled the bill," he said. "Are you ready?"

I nodded, not trusting myself to speak.

He motioned for me to walk in front of him, and obligingly, I led the way to the front of the restaurant. Our coats were brought promptly, and I stepped outside with mine folded over my arm. From the doorway, I could see the Bentley waiting to whisk me back to the University of Maryland.

I didn't want to go.

Mr. Thorne's hand rested lightly on the small of my back as he guided me down the iron stairs. Even through the thickness of the satin blouse, his cool fingers burned against my flesh. As I reached the sidewalk, I couldn't stop myself. I turned into his arm, so that I was facing him, my body a hand's breadth from his.

From there, I could smell his personal scent, under the sandalwood and musk. I was excruciatingly aware of him, aware of the weight deep in my belly and the wetness between my legs. I ached for him. I couldn't move.

"Please," I said, the word escaping. I was trapped in his spell, and only he could release me.

"You do not know what you are asking for," he said, his voice rough. The hand that still rested on my back became rigid.

"I wouldn't care if I did, and you know it," I whispered, looking up into that beautiful, impossible face.

His head came forward then, his lips parting, and

for one interminable moment, I thought he was going to kiss me. But abruptly, he shifted his hold on me and held me at arm's length as he turned his face away.

"And that," he said, "is exactly why I won't."

With that, he bundled me into the car, shutting the door with devastating finality. He stood on the sidewalk, his brow furrowed and his hands thrust into his pockets, as the Bentley rolled away. And I watched him until the car turned a corner and he disappeared from my sight.

CHAPTER EIGHT

"Cora!" Lisette's exclamation stopped me in the doorway. "Thank God. I was about to call the police!"

I looked around our living room. Lisette had roused half the apartment complex. Sarah, Hannah, Emily, and Sabrina were waiting with various expressions of relief and outrage on their faces. Even Christina and Chelsea were there, lounging in the corner in skintight shirts and their clubbing makeup.

Sarah was talking on the phone. "Yeah, you can come back up. She's here. She's okay."

"What's going on?" I asked.

"What is wrong with you?" Lisette demanded. "Why didn't you answer your phone? You left four hours ago. We thought something horrible had happened to you."

"Oh, crap," I said, seized by guilt. I fumbled in my clutch and pulled out my phone. I'd missed eight calls, mostly Lisette's. "Twenty-four texts, guys? Really?"

"No one knew where you were," Sarah said, hanging up. "Geoff saw you get into some rich dude's car. Lisette thought you'd be back in a couple of hours. When nine o'clock rolled around and you still weren't answering your phone...."

"Lisette said your new doctor is really sketch," Hannah said. "You didn't tell her where you were going. He could have been some kind of serial killer rapist or something."

"Seriously, though, he could have been really dangerous," Lisette said.

I sank onto a corner of the couch, edging Sabrina to the side. I felt emptied, hollowed out, and my finger was throbbing.

They were right. So very right. Mr. Thorne was the most dangerous man I'd ever met. And his interest in me, for whatever reason, was far more intense than scientific attentiveness could possibly account for.

"I'm so sorry, guys. The meeting ran long, and I had my ringer off, and I was so tired afterward that I forgot to check my calls."

Lisette's face softened instantly. She always forgave easily. "It's just that it's not like you to disappear for so long. If it had been Chelsea or Christina—"

"You know we're sitting right here," Chelsea said, lobbing a pillow at Lisette's head.

The girls all laughed, and I joined in, terror and regret and relief somehow all spilling out at once. The tension dissipated.

Slumping back against the couch cushions, I thought about it for a minute. I said, "Wait. You all thought some guy had me locked up in his torture dungeon or something, and you thought the smart thing to do then was to huddle in our apartment? And, what, send Mike to walk around campus looking for me?"

"Shut up, Cora," Emily said, running her hand through her cropped hair. "You'd be a lot more embarrassed if you'd come back to find that we'd called the campus cops."

"I'm glad you've got my back," I said, completely deadpan. "Otherwise, I could be in some serious trouble."

This time, the pillow was thrown at me.

After another round of hugs and threats, Emily, Hannah, Sarah, and Sabrina headed back to their rooms, and Christina and Chelsea grabbed their purses and headed out to for the frat party that they'd heard about—all the hardcore partiers started Thursday night, since that homework wasn't due until the next Tuesday.

Then Lisette and I were alone in the apartment. She looked suddenly tired, and with a jolt of guilt, I knew it was my fault. She'd borne too much of the weight of my illness. She made sure that I ate when I was too wrung out to care, coaxed me to my classes on my bad days, and even threw half a load of my laundry in with hers when my pile got too high.

If anyone deserved to know everything, it was Lisette. But I didn't know how much I could tell her. So much had happened that I didn't understand myself, and most of what I could tell her would only worry her more because none of it fit into Lisette's black-and-white world.

"What did the doctor say?" Lisette asked.

"I actually spoke to the CEO," I said. "He said I was a good candidate. He went through the procedure and outlined the risks."

"And?" Lisette prompted.

"And you were right. The risks are really high. But I'm going to tell him yes." I shrugged. "Even a slim chance is better than none at all. And I'm not ready to call hospice."

Her expression was fierce. "You shouldn't be. Well, good for you. When will the drug trial start?"

"It's more of a single-dose thing," I said. "In two weeks, I can call and make an appointment. If it works, the results should be pretty immediate."

"And if it doesn't?" Lisette asked.

I shrugged. "I'm dying, anyway. There's not much worse than that."

Lisette made a face. She hated when I talked about death. "That won't happen," she said confidently.

And however foolishly, I felt sure that she was right.

"So," I said, changing the subject, "you worried about me being gone for four hours, but you let C-and-C walk out of here dressed like that, knowing just what kind of trouble they're headed into, without a word of protest?"

"Eh," Lisette said with a dismissive shake of her head. "They went nuts the day they turned twenty-one. Worrying about them is kind of pointless now. Besides, they've got each other. More or less." She raised her eyebrows. "And if I lost you, I'd have to find another study partner."

Lisette didn't like doing homework alone—that's how we'd first become friends—but I knew she was perfectly capable of keeping her 4.0 without my help. She was just making sure that, however tired I was, I got the work done, too.

I sank deeper into the sofa and kicked off my shoes with a groan. I couldn't even think about getting up. I couldn't physically do it.

"Fine, I'll take the hint, but I'm not moving from this couch," I said, playing along. "If you want to go over the homework, you'll have to bring my work to me."

"Deal," Lisette said, disappearing into my bedroom.

Left alone, I looked at my aching, blistered finger and thought about what I had said about being locked up in a torture chamber. I had been joking at the time, but I realized that it was very possible with this man. But with him, I would tie myself up and apply the instruments of torture to my own flesh...and be glad.

I hugged myself, sick with horror at how very plausible that thought was, and even more sick at the thought that part of me, even now, would welcome such a fate.

CHAPTER NINE

I t was Tuesday of the next week when a call across McKeldin Mall stopped me in my tracks.

"Hey, Shaw!"

I turned around to see Geoff grinning at me in the slightly worried way I'd come to dread.

Oh, damn. Someone had told him that I was sick. Now I was going to find out just how much he knew.

"Hi, Geoff," I said, pausing so that he could catch up more quickly. I mostly took the bus to travel between my south campus apartment and my classes now, but I wasn't heading home quite yet.

"Headed to lunch?" he asked.

"Yeah," I said. "I've got some extra Terp Bucks to burn before finals are over, so I was going to The

Dairy." The Dairy had a decent selection of sandwiches, pizza, and, of course, ice cream made on site, and with my dining money expiring at the end of the term, it was time to use it or lose it.

"Me, too," he said. "Join you?"

"Sure," I said.

We walked along in an awkward silence for a couple of minutes. I watched Geoff out of the corner of my eye. He was visibly struggling, trying to come up with a polite way to ask me about being sick.

I sighed and stopped, turning toward him. He took one more step forward before he realized that I was not beside him anymore.

"So, what have you heard?" I asked. "And who did you hear it from, because I want to know who I should kill?"

Geoff looked uncomfortable. "Cancer?" he said. "For real?"

I let out a puff of air and started walking again. I was too tired for this. "Yeah. For real," I said.

"I thought you'd gotten some kind of eating disorder or something," he said. "I mean, your hair—"

"Yeah, thanks, you and half the world," I said. "It's the wrong kind of cancer to be treated with chemo that causes all your hair to fall out."

"So, you mean like...." He made a vague cupping motion at chest level.

I punched him in the arm. "Seriously, what is wrong with guys? You find out I have cancer, and the first thing you think about is my tits? Really?"

"Well, what other kind of cancer do girls get?" he

said, but he was grinning now.

"That had better be a joke," I said. I knew it was. And if Geoff could crack a joke, I might survive this conversation. "And no, my boobs are fine. It's leukemia. And the first treatment didn't work, so my doctor's going to have me on something new soon."

"But you're going to be okay, right?" Geoff's face went serious. "We were getting along so well at the end of last year, and then when this semester started, I thought we'd be able to pick up where we'd left off...."

I felt a pang of guilt. I'd gone on my first date with Geoff four days before I got my diagnosis. "Yeah. Sorry about that. I guess I kinda shut down for a while."

"I thought our date went well, myself," Geoff said.

"Oh, it did," I assured him. "I'm still a terrible bowler. But it was fun. It's just...with everything I had to deal with...."

We had reached The Dairy. Geoff grabbed the door and held it open for me as I went inside.

"Look, it wasn't you. It was just crappy timing. We weren't really dating yet, and I couldn't dump all this in your lap, and I felt like, if we kept going out, I'd be lying to you if I hid it." We joined the back of the line.

"So you thought it'd be better to ignore me," he said. "Instead of letting me decide what I could handle. It wasn't like we'd just met. I'd known you for three years. I considered you a friend. I still consider you a friend."

He had a point. "I consider you a friend, too. I didn't want you to think that I was trying to make you be something more, throwing it all on you after one date."

"It still wasn't your decision," he said. "At least, it wasn't only your decision."

By then, we'd made it to the register. I made my order, and so did Geoff. He added my food to his tray and led the way to a table in the corner of the dining area, and I took the chair across from him, dropping my bag under my chair. I tried not to show how grateful I was to give my tired legs a break. He set my sandwich and drink in front of me.

"Thanks," I said.

Geoff leaned forward. "You know, I was beginning to wonder if I really was that bad of a kisser."

I felt the heat rise in my face, and I fiddled with my sandwich to cover it. "Not at all," I said. It was my turn to feel awkward. "It was nice."

At the end of our date, he had dropped me off at my apartment door. The hall lights had been turned to their nighttime setting, only half the fluorescent tubes on so as not to glare into the apartments when someone opened a door. I was leaning against the door. The corridor emptied for a moment as we talked, and he stepped up, so quickly that it caught my breath, and cupped the back of my head in his hand.

"I've been wanting to do this for a long time," he had said, and then his mouth came down over mine, and I had tipped my face up to meet him. His mouth was hot, hard and soft at once, and a warm delicious ness unspiraled inside me. Clutching his shirt, I opened my lips under his.

When the kiss finally ended and he stepped back, I

looked away, breathless and blushing furiously.

"Um," I said. "Whoa. Sorry. I didn't mean to eat your face off. I hope I didn't scare you."

He chuckled, and I shivered slightly. My heart was still beating too hard. "Trust me, Cora. I'm not scared." He took a lock of my hair and pushed it back over my shoulder. "See you?" he asked, and I knew he didn't mean in class.

"Yeah," I said. "Absolutely."

Then he had left me to fumble into my apartment and collapse on the couch, hoping we hadn't just ruined a friendship trying for something more.

"Nice?" Geoff said now, settling back with an exaggerated air of disgust. "That's all I get? Nice?"

"Okay, better than nice," I admitted. "I was looking forward to going out again." I took a bite.

"Well, good. Because so was I," he said, shifting with his usual swiftness back to seriousness again.

"I'm sorry," I repeated. "It just wasn't a good time for me to get into anything new."

"And now?" he asked. He raised his eyebrows over his slice of pizza.

It was striking how different he was from Mr. Thorne, I thought inanely. Geoff was boyish and golden, with light honey-brown hair and a perpetual tan that he got from hours on the lacrosse field. He was sporty without being a jock, with a self-effacing humor that never failed to make me smile. I was still a bit dazzled that he was interested in me. It wasn't that I was unpretty or anything. I just didn't have the sparkling kind of personality or background that usually attracted guys like him. I was the wingman to Lisette's charm.

In contrast, Mr. Thorne was cold and remote, arrogant and God-only-knows how much older. I couldn't even picture him where Geoff was, sitting in the humming Dairy, legs outstretched and a negligent half-grin on his face.

I shook my head. Mr. Thorne, I told myself, was not a possible...boyfriend. I didn't know what he was—I still couldn't wrap my head around it—but he was a creature of another world entirely.

"After Winter Break," I said, answering Geoff's question. "I'll know by then if the new treatment is working."

"And if it isn't?" Geoff said, his forehead creasing with concern. He set the pizza down.

"If it isn't, I won't be around long enough to make a relationship worth it," I said bluntly.

He looked stricken. "Shaw—"

"Please, don't. I can't deal with that right now. After the break. I'm sure I'll be doing better then," I said, making promises I had no power to keep. I finished half of my sandwich.

"But we're still on for studying for finals together, right?" he asked. Geoff had been a part of Lisette's economics study group from our first meeting, and he was the only other one who still met with us before each test.

"As long as Lisette's along to chaperone, sure." I smiled at him, picking up the second half of my sandwich.

"Like she'll let you study without her," he said.

"She's the one I have to kill, isn't she?" I asked. "She told you I was sick."

He looked uncomfortable. "I asked. She didn't want to tell me at first."

"But she did," I said. "Oh, well. I'm sure she thought it was for the best. She always does."

"She's a good friend, Shaw," he said.

"I know she is." A better friend than I deserved. I finished my sandwich. "And since she's the one who told you about my cancer, she should be the one to have to put up with all the *tension* between us." I said the word with deliberately exaggerated drama.

"You don't trust me?" he demanded.

"Maybe," I said, standing up and gathering up my trash and my bag, "I don't trust me."

With another grin over my shoulder, I threw away the trash and ducked out of The Dairy, feeling lighter than I had in days and leaving Geoff gaping at the table behind me.

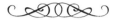

CHAPTER TEN

A week later, I wasn't feeling so optimistic. I had come down with a cold that had turned into a raging ear and sinus infection, and I was trying to gut it out and push through the last week of school before finals. I had been feeling so much better without the side effects of the alemtuzumab that I had almost managed to put out of my mind how sick I really was. But feeling better or not, I wasn't healing. I was, slowly, inevitably, getting worse.

Dr. Robeson had hammered the seriousness of this kind of illness into me the first time I'd seen her. Opportunistic infections were a leading cause of death for victims of leukemia, she'd said—it was my white blood cells that were broken, so even as they multiplied out of

control, they stopped doing their job of fighting inva-
sions, large and small. If an infection didn't kill me, then
I could look forward to hemorrhage, catastrophic gastric
ulceration, or drowning in my own fluids with pulmo-
nary edema.

Good times.

I called Dr. Robeson as soon as I recognized the
signs of another infection. She prescribed me a round of
ciprofloxacin over the phone. The infection could be
viral, she explained, but waiting for a culture could
lower the chances of the antibiotics being effective if
was bacterial, given my compromised immune system.
It was my third infection since I had been diagnosed
with leukemia—and the second time I'd heard that spiel.

"Have you called to hospice?" she asked. "You
don't have to choose that path, but I do wish you'd at
least talk to them."

"No," I said. "And I'm not going to. I called the
other number that you gave me. The card."

There was silence on the other end of the phone
for a moment. "And how did that go?"

"It went well," I said. "I think. I passed the screening. I'm supposed to call in two days and give my
consent for the procedure." I had tried again to look up
anything I could online, but the name *Thorne* and a
phone number weren't enough to give me any relevant
hits. "Can you tell me about this company? Its name?
The CEO's background?"

"I'm afraid I really can't," Dr. Robeson said. "But I
trust Mr. Thorne implicitly."

"The treatment is risky," I said. "It probably won't

work."

"I know," said Dr. Robeson.

"But if it's the only chance I have...." I let that trail off.

"Cora, there's nothing more I or any other oncologist can do. Mr. Thorne's procedure, however unorthodox, is your only possibility of a cure." Her voice wasn't unkind, but she was firm.

I let out the breath I didn't know I had been holding. "Thanks for being blunt. I needed the reassurance. My judgment...." I trailed off, then changed the subject. "I'd really already decided to go for it. Anyway, I'll be picking up the antibiotics at the Health Center, as usual."

"I'll call it in. Goodbye, Cora," she said. "And good luck."

"Bye," I said, and I hung up.

And that was that.

I grabbed the picture that sat on my bedside table and turned it so I could see it from the bed. In the photo, I was grinning and holding up my high school diploma with my Gramma's arm wrapped around my shoulders in a fierce hug. She looked so happy. Triumphant, even. She'd done it, giving me a normal childhood all on her own after my parents' death in the car accident. She'd put off her retirement for more than ten years, I found out later, to support me. *Worked herself to death*, a small voice whispered. I could never pay her back, but I'd wanted to succeed to show her that all her sacrifice had meant something. If Mr. Thorne's experimental procedure didn't work, I'd be dead in less than a semester.

Logically, I knew my chances were slim, but I was convinced that this time, I would be the one-in-one-hundred lucky one. I don't know where that conviction came from, but no amount of rational thought could shake it.

I levered myself out of bed and dragged on some clothes. My head felt like it was stuffed with a wad of cotton, my sinuses were slowly burning through my skull, and my ear throbbed dully. I wavered for a moment, wondering if I could even make it to class. I looked at my Gramma, eternally beaming from the photo, and I sighed. Shoving my feet into my UGG knockoffs, I went into the kitchen and poured myself a bowl of cereal.

"Hey, Cora," Lisette said from the living room. "I thought you'd left for class."

"No," I said, splashing milk over my raisin bran. I was glad to see her even though I'd pay for our conversation later that day, when my endurance gave out. A year ago, I could never have imagined how many thousands of small costs of strength there were in a day, how each and every action I took exacted its own toll.

I flopped in a chair and dug in. I hadn't gained any weight back since stopping the alemtuzumab, but I hadn't lost any more, either, for a change. "I had to call Dr. Robeson and get another script for cipro. I can't shake this ear infection."

"I'm sorry. Have you seen Geoff since our last study session?" she asked with exaggerated casualness.

I aimed my spoon at her. "I know it was you who

told him I'm sick, so don't play innocent with me. He admitted it."

"Wait, he talked to you? And you didn't tell me?" She looked betrayed.

"Last week. And I didn't tell you because you opened your big mouth and told him about my cancer."

"Oh, come on, Cora. He's been mooning after you all semester," Lisette said. "And you weren't going to do anything about it. Somebody had to."

"It's my life," I grumbled.

"And it's his, too," she pointed out. "Anyhow, you've been weird ever since you came back from your last appointment with Dr. Robeson. It's not healthy."

"I'm not healthy," I returned.

"So, what did Geoff say?" Lisette was not to be distracted. "Dish! I can't believe you guys have been studying with me for three days now, and I had no idea."

I sighed. "He's still interested, okay? And believe it or not, so am I."

Lisette made an absurd squealing noise, and I treated her to a glare.

"After Christmas," I said. "If the treatment's worked."

"So you're going to go for the treatment? For sure?" Lisette asked.

"Yeah," I said. "I can call and make my appointment in two days. As soon as finals are over, I'm doing it."

"I know you'll pull through," Lisette said staunchly. "It's going to work. It's got to."

"Yeah," I said.

I hesitated for a moment. I didn't want to hurt her. I didn't want my memory to hurt her. She already cared far too much, far more than I deserved. But there were things I had to say. Just in case.

I said, "But if I don't—"

"You will!" Lisette said sharply.

"*Listen*," I said. "If I don't, I just want to say...thanks. For everything. You're the best friend I could ever have, and I've been a pretty shitty one these last two years, with Gramma and then the leukemia."

Her face crumpled. "Don't you dare say that, Cora Shaw. You're my best friend, too. You're like the sister I never had."

I laughed at that, dispelling the tears that had begun to prick my eyes. "But you have a sister. Actually at UMD, in fact."

She smiled with palpable relief. "Yeah, but you're not like that one. So, after Christmas?" she prompted, steering the conversation back to safer shores.

"Then Geoff and I try to pick up where we left off. More or less."

She rolled her eyes. "Where you left off was making longing faces at each other over your textbooks and lunch trays. You've got to do better than that."

"You're one to talk, little miss no-love-life," I returned.

"At least I'm not making all my friends sit through my ridiculously protracted mating ritual," she said. "Seriously, you're like a middle schooler."

I finished my bowl of cereal, dumped out the milk,

and set the bowl in the sink to wash after lunch. "I'm not really the rushing type," I said. I pulled on my jacket and swung my backpack over my shoulder.

"It's been three years, Cora. I don't think anybody's going to accuse you of rushing," said Lisette.

"I'll see you tonight," I said pointedly, my hand on the door.

She smiled. "Yeah, see you."

I was alone in the room, some kind of stone chamber with supporting arches every few feet that made it impossible to see very far.

"Hello?" I called out.

There was no answer.

The room was cold. I rubbed my palms against my upper arms, the muscles of my stomach and nipples tightening beneath the thigh-length tee shirt that was my only clothing. I began walking, peering through the murky dimness, moving through the maze of pillar and arch aimlessly. I had to reach a wall eventually, I decided. Somewhere, there had to be an end to this.

Then I saw the light. It was red, low, and fitful, but it gave me a destination, and I sped up, my bare feet soft on the bare dirt floor. I came around a final pillar, and I saw it then, a kind of metal bowl or fire pit full of coals so hot that they were nearly smokeless, bending the air above them with their heat.

I approached, drawn by the warmth in the dank chill of the endless chamber.

And then I saw him. And my heart seemed to stop.

Mr. Thorne stood in the shadows on the other side of the fire. He was nothing like the urbane, contained man I had sat across from at the restaurant. Dressed in a loose white shirt and dark pants, he seemed larger, freer, and not entirely human.

"Ms. Shaw." My name sounded like a prayer on his lips. Those lips, slightly, wickedly fuller than they should be. "You've come."

I said nothing, mesmerized by his raw beauty.

He circled the fire pit in slow, stalking steps. He was dragging something at his side, something long and narrow, but I could not take my eyes off his face to look at it properly.

He came right up to me and stopped, just as he had when I'd turned to face him in front of the restaurant. Then he pulled me against him with one hand, so that I could feel the length of his body, and his mouth came down over mine.

And I lost myself. The heat flared up in my midsection, twisting inside me, lancing down between my thighs and up, into my lungs and into my heart until I could only cling to him.

Then I felt him pressing something into my palm. His other hand, the one that held the object. And I saw that it was a long, thin rod of iron, and on the end of it was a letter: T. His letter.

His brand.

"Take it, Ms. Shaw." He breathed the words into my hair.

My hand closed around the rod. I knew what he wanted, and I knew that I would do it. My heart beat wildly out of control.

Mr. Thorne kissed me again, urgently, and I stuck the end into the coal. I threw back my head as his kisses moved lower, across my neck, to the collar of the tee shirt. His free hand skimmed over my body, up from my thigh, under the shirt, and then he was pulling it off over my head. I was naked in front of him, but I was too hungry to be ashamed.

He said, "It is time."

He stepped back, and I kept my eyes fixed on him, rejoicing as I reached for the end of the iron rod. The brand was glowing red from the blistering coals.

I knew what he wanted. His eyes filled my world. I grasped the rod of the brand as close to the heated end as I could bear. I turned it toward me, toward my naked flesh, shivering in terror and desire.

And he didn't even have to ask.

I pressed the brand against my abdomen, and the stench of the burning flesh filled my nostrils as the terrible, glorious agony of it swept over me—

And my own scream woke me.

I was sitting up in bed, the blankets kicked off onto the floor, the alarm of my phone blaring at full volume. Still panting and shuddering with reaction, I groped for the off button, and then I scrubbed my face with the heels of my hands.

Thursday. It was the Thursday before finals—

exactly two weeks after I had seen Mr. Thorne at Komi.

No wonder I was having nightmares.

I took a breath and lurched into the bathroom. A shower chased away the last of the dream, leaving me with a clearer head.

Decision time.

Dammit, I'd made my decision. I'd made it two weeks ago—before that, even, back at Johns Hopkins, when I'd chosen the mysterious card over the hospice brochure.

I glared at my thin body in the mirror, glared at the ravages the cancer had done upon it. My hip bones protruded, stark and angry, my ribs an ugly line of bars, my cheeks sunken and eyes hollow. I was going to take the leap of faith. Even if I landed on crumbling ground, I already knew the bridge I stood on now was doomed.

I wrapped up in the towel, went back into my room, and grabbed the phone from the bedside table. I searched for the number that I had stored under the contact *LAST HOPE*. I hit send.

"Cora Shaw," came the familiar voice of the man who attended the phone. "We have been expecting your call."

"Yes," I said. My voice shook slightly, and I swallowed hard. "I am ready to give my answer."

"That is good to hear, Ms. Shaw. What shall I tell Mr. Thorne?"

I opened my mouth, but no sound came out.

"Ms. Shaw?"

I heard my voice answer as if from very far away. "I want to go through the procedure. Next Friday, after my finals."

"A car can pick you up at six. Will that be acceptable, Ms. Shaw?"

"Very," I said. "Thank you."

"No, thank *you*, Ms. Shaw."

The line went dead.

I'd done it. I was committed.

I put my hand to my chest, so I could feel the frantic rhythm of my heart, which circulated my poisoned blood with every beat. In eight days, it would be purified, rid of the mutant cells that threatened to overwhelm my body even as they failed in its defense.

Or else I would die.

Either way, I would see Mr. Thorne again. And I would know which of my fears were imagined and which were very, very real.

.

CHAPTER ELEVEN

"That's it! Last final!" Lisette let out a whoop and slammed her textbook into the nearest trash can. "Take that, econometrics!"

"You know you could have sold that back," I pointed out. "And anyway, it's not like you even hated the course."

She grinned. "A new edition was published two months ago, and now the university bookstore and Amazon won't pay jack for this one. I've been wanting to do that for three and a half years, but this is the first time one of my textbooks became obsolete the same semester I was using it."

"That kind of defeats the purpose of a grand gesture," Geoff said. "I mean, if it's trash, anyway...."

"Shut up," she said cheerfully. "Let's celebrate." She spied someone else across the green. "Hey, Ross! Sabrina! Come on, let's celebrate!"

Sabrina waved, and they crossed over. "You guys done?" Sabrina asked. Ross Myo had been an economics major, too, before switching to statistics his sophomore year. He'd met Sabrina, a bio major, in the taekwondo club, and she'd become a fixture in our group when we got together.

"They are—until next semester," Geoff said, nodding at me and Lisette. "I've still got a history final in three hours. It's no biggie, though. 100-level core course that I saved for my senior year slack-off."

"When are you guys taking off for break?" Lisette asked.

"Our plane doesn't leave until tomorrow." Sabrina cast a look at Ross. "I'm meeting the 'rents."

"'Rents? Who the heck says 'rents?" Lisette said cheerfully. "I've got to be home by dinner, but my car's already packed, so I've got..." She checked her watch. "Two and a half hours to burn." Lisette lived just outside of Baltimore, in the tony suburb of Ellicott City.

"So what do you want to do?" I asked.

"I don't know. What do young people do these days?" Lisette said, rolling her eyes.

"You know that we're just going to end up playing ping pong at the Stamp," Geoff said.

"Table tennis, please," said Ross in a pained voice.

"You just want it to sound cooler because you always beat us," I said.

"Freaking Asians and their table tennis," Sabrina said, grinning at her Korean boyfriend as they linked arms.

Lisette let out a huff of air. "Fine, then. Be boring. It's not like I have hours to burn figuring out what we're going to do." She stalked toward the Adele H. Stamp Student Union with exaggerated exasperation.

Sabrina chuckled, brushing her thick, straight blonde hair back out of her face. "She's full of something today."

"Final high," I said. "She aced everything. Makes her kind of slap-happy."

We entered the Stamp, and Lisette led us down the stairs, talking ninety miles an hour the whole way. When we arrived at the TerpZone student activity center, it was mostly empty. Half the students had already gone home.

"You do realize that we're celebrating leaving school for two weeks by hanging out...at school," I said as Geoff paid for a table.

"Oh, hush," said Lisette. "Better than sitting around, doing nothing." She snatched up the ball and one of the paddles. "Who's gonna face me first? I am invincible! Except you, Ross, because you'll beat me," she added.

Geoff smiled at me over her head. "I paid. Other paddle is mine."

"He'll beat you, too," I predicted.

"Have some faith!" Lisette protested.

I grabbed one of the chairs and sat gratefully behind Geoff as he returned Lisette's serve. My legs ached dully, echoed by my head. I never wanted to move again.

I liked watching him—tall, rangy, and athletic. And the rear view wasn't too shabby, either. I could tell that he wasn't really putting his attention into the game, but he still beat Lisette handily.

"Your turn?" he asked, offering the paddle to me.

I shook my head, forcing a smile. "I'm a bit tired."

In all honesty, I could not have kept up with either of them for a minute, trying or no. My ear infection had all but cleared up, but the stress of finals on top of the leukemia had left me wrung out.

"Come on," Lisette groaned. "Now I'm going to be the ping pong dummy."

"Table tennis," Sabrina corrected, grabbing the paddle from Geoff.

"You have an unfair advantage," Lisette said, pointing her paddle accusingly at Sabrina. "Your boyfriend has been showing you all those Asian table tennis secrets."

Sabrina grinned. "Damned right. And I'm gonna school the rest of you whiteys in how it's done."

"Learning to play ping pong doesn't make you any less white," Lisette sniffed. "And it won't make Ross's grandmother like you one bit more."

Sabrina served, and Lisette ducked as the ball bounced once and whizzed straight for her, letting out a piercing shriek.

Geoff and Ross whooped and Sabrina growled in mock fierceness, waving her paddle threateningly as Lisette scrambled after the ball. I laughed so hard that tears sprang to my eyes, my sides aching. It had been so long since I'd laughed, really laughed, that I'd almost forgotten what it was like.

Lisette brought back the ball and threw it at Sabrina, who caught it easily. Geoff grinned down at me, hauling another chair beside mine. He flopped into it. It was nice to have him near.

I snaked out a hand, half-hidden, under the arm of the chair. He took it and folded it in his own. It felt good.

Over the next ten minutes, Sabrina crushed Lisette, who surrendered her paddle to Ross. "I'm not even going to try against you," she said.

Ross and Sabrina played a couple of games while we watched, Ross spending as much time coaching Sabrina as playing against her. After his win, Lisette insisted that Sabrina and Geoff have a final showdown, to see how much Ross's instruction had improved her game since we'd played together last. This time, Geoff was on his toes, lunging and jumping to return Sabrina's volleys. A fast one whizzed by, and he threw himself back to catch it.

"Watch out!" Sabrina yelled, but it was too late. He slammed into my chair, and we both went over in a tangle.

"And game," she said, coming around the table to help.

Geoff had put out his hand at the last minute to keep his weight from landing squarely on me, but I'd hit the ground hard enough to knock the wind out of me.

"Crap, Shaw," he said, jumping up. He slipped an

arm under mine and pulled me to my feet. "I'm so sorry. I forgot you were there. I mean, I knew you were there, but I didn't know I was that close."

I clung to his arm for a moment to steady myself. He looked so guilt-stricken, his broad face earnest and intent.

"Really, I'm fine, Geoff," I reassured him. "I'm not that fragile." I let go of him, and a moment later, he released me cautiously.

"Thanks for the win, Cora," Sabrina said. "The old stationary-chair trick gets them every time."

"Very funny, Sabrina," I said, making a face at her. "I've got to go anyway, guys. I've got an appointment tonight, so I was planning on catching a nap before I leave."

"Sure, no problem," Sabrina said casually. She and Ross didn't know that I was sick.

"Good luck, and *call me*," Lisette said intently. She gave me a worried smile. "In case you're asleep when I stop by and I can't say goodbye."

"I'll walk you," Geoff said, picking up my book bag. "I need to do some last minute reviewing, anyway."

"Sure," I said. "Bye, guys."

"Bye," Lisette said. She waggled her eyebrows dramatically, looking at Geoff and back at me. I scowled at her. Geoff had the good grace to pretend not to notice the exchange.

Geoff and I walked side by side, not exactly comfortably, but I wouldn't say the slight awkwardness was a bad thing, either. It was an awareness of his closeness, his golden looks, and his size, relative to mine.

"You sure you're okay?" he asked.

"I'm fine," I assured him again. He looked so worried that I couldn't help myself. "All except my ankle, but I'm sure that will heal in a few weeks."

"Shaw—" he began, his face a mask of guilt.

I relented instantly. "Kidding. Totally kidding."

"That wasn't funny," he muttered as he opened the door for me to precede him outside.

"Was to me," I said.

He just shook his head.

"Are you seriously going to carry my books for me all the way back to my dorm, like in some kind of cornball TV show?" I asked.

"Would you like me to?" he returned.

I smiled. "I wouldn't mind." In truth, the backpack had felt heavier than it had any right to feel, dragging at my whole body after the end of the grueling week of tests.

"Are you going to Lisette's place again this Christmas?" he asked, changing the subject.

I shook my head. "I'm starting the new therapy tonight, and staying here will give me time to recover. Anyhow, I've already paid for housing over the break."

"I'm leaving as soon as my last final is over," he said. "My family's expecting me home before dinner, too, and with rush hour traffic...." He lived in Annapolis, which was an hour away when the Beltway wasn't crowded.

"Cutting it close?" I asked.

"What can I say? I like to live dangerously. Just yesterday, I reparked my car without fastening my seat belt."

Dangerous. An image of Mr. Thorne came to me then, holding my finger to his lips. I shivered.

"Cold?" Geoff asked.

"No, I'm fine," I said. We got to the front door of the campus apartments. I stopped and turned to him. "Thanks for walking me," I said.

"I'll come up with you," he said, reaching past me to open the door. The casualness of the offer was a little forced. "If I'm carrying your books, I might as well do a proper job of it and take them all the way to your room."

"Sure." I felt my face heat a little, and I ducked under his arm into the building.

"You heard back from any grad schools yet?" I asked as we waited for the elevator.

"Three," he said. "Acceptances from Chicago and Berkley and a rejection from Stanford, but no news yet on assistantships or fellowships. You?"

The elevator doors opened with a chime, and we stepped inside.

"Honestly?" I said, pushing the button for the fourth floor. "I didn't apply until November."

"Ouch," he said.

"I know, stupid, right? But I was distracted. Hope all the slots aren't filled before they look at my application."

Distracted. That was an understatement. I hadn't been physically capable of completing the paperwork. It had taken all the strength I had to make it through my classes.

The doors opened, and we walked to my door, marked by the huge collage of pet memes that Lisette had papered it with. I grabbed the lanyard around my neck and unlocked it, pushing the door open.

"Well, thanks again," I said, extending an arm to take my backpack.

Geoff stepped forward instead, dropping my bag just inside the door. I stepped back automatically, but he caught up with me and pulled my body into his, one arm wrapped around my waist, the other hand tangled in my hair, puffy jackets bunched up between us. I realized his intentions just as his mouth met mine, and instantly, instinctively, I kissed him back.

I leaned into him, letting my sick and weary muscles surrender to his warm strength. I gasped against his lips as his tongue touched my teeth, and I let him urge them apart.

Finally, after a time that was both far too long and far too short, he pulled away. I staggered back a couple of steps and stared at him. He was looking at me, his breath ragged and two spots of color high in his cheeks.

"Well," I said breathlessly. "I did say next semester."

"I know," he said. "And I meant to wait. But I had to say—" He broke off.

"Goodbye," I finished. "But it won't be goodbye. The therapy will work, and we'll both be back in a month, and we'll laugh about how sick and scared I was."

"I'll never laugh at that," he said. His smile was rueful. "But I really do have to cram for my history final."

I grinned back, still feeling the pull of him but more on my own balance again. "And I do need my nap. Go on, then," I said.

"See you in January," he said.

"See you," I returned.

He raised a hand in salute as he stepped backwards, out of the door, and I mirrored him.

Then he was gone.

No longer needing to keep up the pretense of strength, I slumped onto the couch, staring at the empty doorway until it closed on the bright lights of the hallway beyond. Geoff slotted so neatly into my life trajectory: the degree, the boyfriend, the job, the marriage, the house, the kids. It was my modest version of "having it all"—what my Gramma had sacrificed so much so I'd have a chance to have. I'd never imagined any other future, though I wasn't on any kind of rushed timetable to get there.

I still wanted Geoff, along with all the rest. I felt my attraction to him every time he was near, and he would still fit well into the rest of my life that was still laid out in its tidy map, if only the cancer would go away. He might not be the one to end up filling the full boyfriend-husband-father sequence. But he could. And that's what I wanted.

But now, when I tried to fix my mind on the bright image of that future, shadows of Mr. Thorne kept intruding on the edges. He was a man who could never fit in my life plan, not in any capacity. Even so, I still wanted him, too, in a way that I'd never wanted anything else.

Perhaps more than I'd wanted anything else, even now, when he was miles away.

And that terrified me.

The microwave clock read two o'clock. I had four hours—only four hours until the appointment that would determine whether that "see you" was a prediction or an empty promise.

Four hours before I saw Mr. Thorne again.

Well, then, I thought, *I'd better get my sleep.*

Chapter Twelve

At precisely 6:32 PM, the Bentley stopped, and the chauffeur walked around and opened my door. I knew because I checked my phone one last time before turning it off and shoving it into my coat pocket.

"Thank you," I murmured. I realized that this might be my last time in the car—in any car.

I shut down that line of thought as I got out. I was not going to die. Not tonight. It was a knowledge that was deeper than reason. One that I had to cling to.

I hadn't paid attention to the city passing in front of the car window, too distracted by my own whirling thoughts. Now I found myself in front of a dense hedge of hollies, easily fifteen feet tall, with only a passage wide enough for the flagstone walk that squeezed between them.

I turned back to look at the chauffeur.

"It is Mr. Thorne's Georgetown home, Ms. Shaw," the man said with a small bow before I had a chance to ask the question aloud.

"I see," I said, even though I didn't.

Mr. Thorne directed medical procedures from his home? It was absurd, but I couldn't manage to be surprised about anything he might do. I walked up the path even as I heard the Bentley door shut behind me and the change in sound of the engine as it rolled away.

I still didn't know the chauffeur's name, and now I might never learn it.

There was no going back.

The house, half glimpsed between the hedges, revealed itself to me as I passed between them. I stopped.

Rich—I'd known that Mr. Thorne must be a very rich man. But this went beyond all my expectations.

I stood at the edge of a formal walled garden, the immaculate lawn clipped short within the boxwood frames that edged the paths. These crossed precisely in the middle of the garden at a tall iron fountain, empty and silent now for winter. The house rose up beyond, its marble façade so pale it glowed in the city lights that turned the night sky orange.

It was a massive baroque reimagining of classical style, complete with a half flight of stairs leading up to the main floor and a wide porch, like a Roman temple, behind the row of great columns. Here and there, a window shone. I wondered just how big the house was—ten thousand square feet? Fifty thousand? It must date from the age of the robber barons, if not before. I could hardly believe that such a home still lay in private hands, even in Georgetown.

I blew out a long breath. I'd spent even longer deciding what to wear this time than I had for the last meeting. I was going in for a medical procedure, I knew, and a likely fatal one at that. The last thing that mattered was what I wore. But I couldn't make myself go in my college girl jeggings. It seemed too important an event for that. It needed to be mark with some kind of ceremony, some level of deliberateness, however small, so I'd chosen my gray dress pants and a silky black turtleneck with care.

Now they seemed like such trivial things to try to attach such meaning to.

I squared my shoulders and mounted the steps to the great double doors.

One swung open before I could knock. A distinguished-looking gentleman with silver hair and a dark suit greeted me with a cordial nod.

"Ms. Shaw," he said.

"Let me guess," I interrupted, unable to help myself. "Mr. Thorne is waiting."

The man—an honest-to-goodness butler? I wondered—treated me to an indulgent smile. "Indeed, Ms. Shaw. And he will see you now. Come this way."

I stepped inside the foyer, a vast landing before a central set of marble stairs that rose up in front of me, wide enough for a dozen people to mount shoulder-to-shoulder. Two more staircases, each half as wide, flanked it, leading down. Under my feet, an elaborate geometry of inlaid marble spread out, dizzying to examine too closely.

I surrendered my coat to the butler, who made it disappear behind a cast bronze door set into the wall on one side.

"This way, if you please, Ms. Shaw," the man said.

He led the way up the stairs, and I followed. I found myself in a kind of antechamber, separated from the main space by a row of broad columns.

"This floor is the piano nobile, Ms. Shaw," the butler said, stopping at the edge of the room.

I gaped.

It looked like the lobby of some extravagant hotel from a classic Hollywood film, all scarlet upholstery, rich woods, and precious oriental rugs. The space was so vast that the room was divided into a dozen different conversational areas with screens and plants, sculptures and furniture groupings. A two-story colonnade surrounded it, each floor at least fifteen feet high, with a wide corridor behind the columns below and a matching mezzanine above. Above the upper colonnade, the room was ringed with a fresco of classical figures in elegant postures.

"A follower of Botticelli, Ms. Shaw," the butler said comfortably, following my gaze. "Brought from Italy by Mr. Thorne many years ago."

Light filtered down from the clerestory windows above, and only then came the ceiling, divided into coffers which were painted in a variety of mythological and biblical themes and hung with sixteen vast and branching chandeliers.

"Ms. Shaw," the butler said politely, rousing me

from my frozen state.

"Coming," I said, still feeling somewhat stunned.

The man led the way behind the colonnade, passing several tall paneled doors before turning down a side corridor that was wider than my room.

"The main east gallery," he said. It was hung with paintings from floor to ceiling—portraits, landscapes, allegorical scenes all in a great jumble, with the only breaks to make spaces for the doors that occasionally interrupted the long walls. I couldn't imagine what it was all worth.

"The surgery," the man finally said, coming to a stop at the last door at the very end of the corridor. I balked for a moment before I remembered that "surgery" was an outdated term for a doctor's office.

The butler opened the door and took one step inside, stepping clear of the doorway.

"Ms. Shaw to see you, Mr. Thorne," he said to someone unseen inside, giving a crisp half-bow.

I stepped through the doorway. The butler left, closing the door behind him.

Far across the checkered marble floor, Mr. Thorne lounged in a high-backed armchair with one ankle hooked over his knee, balancing a thin laptop on his leg. He was magnificent and immaculate, as always, dressed in a dark gray suit that molded perfectly to his wide shoulders and tapered down to his hips, his refined features inhumanly perfect under his dark wave of hair. Only dimly did I take in the rest of the room—the clusters of potted plants in the corners, the sparse pieces of elegant furniture, the chaise longue that had a sudden, ominous significance.

He shut the laptop and set it on a side table, surveying me as I entered. My breath caught, my heart already beginning to speed up. His look had a half-hidden hunger that defied his impersonal smile.

"Very good, Ms. Shaw. I see that you made it," he said, standing and crossing over to where I stood, frozen. He seemed different now, in his own home. Older, though older than what I couldn't say. Stronger. Darker.

"I said I would come."

He was very close now, and he seemed to be expecting something. Yes. A meeting. That's what this was, I thought. I should shake his hand.

I thrust a hand at him. He took it in his cool grasp, holding it for a lingering moment before completing the shake of greeting and dropping it again.

It was enough to send a rich, shivering reaction through my body and down into my center. Unaccountably, I thought of the kiss Geoff had given me and the terrible dream I'd had a week ago, and I wondered what it would be like to be kissed by this man.

Would I even survive it?

"Is there something that I need to sign?" I asked. "Paperwork to fill out?"

"Not at all," he said. "I am so glad you came."

I wouldn't—couldn't—have missed it for anything.

He took my elbow, and I found myself subtly leaning into him without meaning to.

"There is a dressing room through here," he said, guiding me to an inconspicuous side door. "You may leave your things on the bench. Then we will be ready to proceed."

"Where is the doctor?" I asked. "And the...procedure room?"

"Do not worry about that, Ms. Shaw." He smiled down at me. "Our treatment does not require the sterility of an operating room, and we have found that our patients are much more comfortable in a less stressful environment."

He opened the door and gently guided me through, his fingers light on the small of my back, sending a hot wave of confusion over me. I couldn't resist.

"Come out when you are ready," he said, and he shut the door, leaving me alone.

CHAPTER THIRTEEN

Facing the blank white door, I realized that Mr. Thorne had only answered half my question. I rocked tensely onto the balls of my feet.

I should leave now, before it was too late. I should stop chasing this dream before it led me to hell.

This was all wrong. Somewhere in the base of my brain, an alarm was jangling, getting louder, screaming out against this place, this man. Who would perform medical procedures in his own home, alone, other than a quack or a butcher? Where were the doctors? The nurses? Their lab coats and stethoscopes and clipboards, their machines that beeped and hissed?

But I knew there were none. Somehow, I had always known it.

Those thoughts were distant and small next to my awareness of the man in the next room. I could hardly hear them over the pounding of my heart. My head was still spinning with seeing him, being near him, my body burning from the ghost of his fingers on my back.

I knew I was about to find out exactly what he wanted from me—what he was, that he could do such impossible things to my mind.

I should get out of there, but I didn't move.

I couldn't.

If I left, I was dead, anyway. Not tonight. Not this week, even. But I wouldn't make it past spring. My life was a road that had been washed out by cancer—a broken dead end with nothing beyond. No way to reach the tidy little future I'd always wanted. The future that would prove to my Gramma that everything she'd done had been worth it.

No matter what happened, this was my only chance. It was my straw to grasp, my one-in-one-hundred shot at life.

If Mr. Thorne had lied to me, I would have believed him. When he spoke, I would believe anything. But I knew he wasn't lying, just as I knew he was there, on the other side of the door. Waiting for me.

And I knew that once I stepped into that room, I would do anything for him. Even give him the life I so desperately wanted to save.

Tearing my gaze from the blank door, I looked around the small, bare room. A narrow padded bench sat against the wall across from a row of pegs, from which a white garment hung limply with a pair of soft white slippers underneath.

I knew what I would do—what I had to do. Mechanically, I stripped down to my skin, folding my clothes and placing them in a neat stack upon the bench, goosebumps springing up over my body.

I pulled the white garment off the hook, expecting the usual ties and buttons of a hospital gown. Instead, it was sewn like a loose, sleeveless dress with a wide boat neck. I slipped it over my head. It hung halfway down my calves, the fabric soft and thick, nothing like the flimsy, stiff hospital gowns I was used to.

My feet were aching from the chill of the marble, and I stuffed them into the slippers. They were, as I knew they would be, a perfect fit.

Then I turned and faced the door. *Run*, a corner of my brain begged, faint and far away. I thought of my promise to Geoff, of Lisette's unwavering support, of graduation and the job and the house and the wedding and the children I didn't yet have.

And then I thought of Mr. Thorne, and the conviction came over me that, one way or another, I was never really going to leave this place.

I felt hollow, like I had been cored out. My stomach and head were light with fear. But I had only one choice. I grasped the door handle, twisted it, and stepped through, back into the surgery.

"Ms. Shaw," Mr. Thorne said, turning toward me in the center of the room.

All it took was the sight of him, with his hungry eyes and beautiful mouth, and my last primal urge to flee abandoned me. *Anything.* I would do anything he wanted of me.

Beside him was the chaise longue, a heavy throw

blanket laid across the foot. That was where I was going to lie for the procedure. I knew it, as certainly as I knew anything. Behind the chaise was a forest of potted plants. The equipment must be back there, somewhere, discreetly hidden away.

A change had come over Mr. Thorne. He seemed taller, even more powerful, as if he had stepped out of some unseen shackles and stretched to his full size, gathering the shadows of the room around him. His gaze was as dark as sin and as inescapable. This was, somehow, the Mr. Thorne of my dream, and my heart, already humming, began to beat harder against my chest.

"Come forward, Ms. Shaw."

The words shook me, blew through me, stripping away every hesitation, every extraneous thought, until all that was left was him. I crossed over to him. I would have walked over broken glass, if he'd asked. I couldn't disobey, and I could see in his eyes that he knew it and was allowing himself the pleasure of it, no longer trying to restrain the hold he had over me.

I stopped with only inches between us. My eyes were held by his gaze. He lifted a hand to my cheek, and I turned into his palm, unbidden, breathing him, my lips tingling against the thick pad of his thumb. My nerves were singing again, singing with awareness of him, with the anticipation of something more.

"You poor child," he murmured, looking down at me, pity and hunger warring in his eyes.

"Please," I said, finding my voice for a moment. "I want to live."

101

He bent his head toward mine, his hand sliding under my hair to cradle my neck. I tipped my head back, my lips parting, as his other hand found the small of my back.

"I want you to live, too," he said, so quietly that I could scarcely hear. "May God have mercy on me."

And then he kissed me.

My vision darkened as his mouth met mine, my legs giving way. His arms tightened around me, holding me easily against the length of his body. Mine was on fire, my nerves sizzling with the touch of him. His mouth—I gave him everything he demanded, welcoming his invasion, tasting him, wanting him, needing him.

His tongue took my mouth. This was no urging, no coaxing. It was an assertion of ownership, and I surrendered to it.

My nipples went hard, chafing against the fabric of my gown. I knew he could feel them through my dress and his shirt, pressed against his chest, and I wanted him to. I wanted him to know how badly I wanted him, how much I craved his touch.

He held me so hard that I could hardly breathe, but I wanted him closer still. His thigh was between my legs, and I knew he could feel the heat that pooled there. I ground my hips into him, gasping against his mouth, and the heat flickered upward and outward, into my center and through my body. He pushed back, hard, and I whimpered with need. His erection was against my hip. I had lost my mind. I didn't care. I just wanted him.

He bent over then, lifting me from my feet, effortlessly laying me on the chaise.

"No," I said as he released me, pulling weakly at his jacket. My skin was burning, the gown an unbearable torture against it. My thighs were wet with my desire.

"Enough," he said, and I had to subside. He reached down to the foot of the chaise and drew the thick blanket over my body. It settled over me, thick and muffling, a wall between our bodies.

No, I want you, I thought, but I could not speak the words. I could see the strain in his body, betraying that he wanted me just as much as I burned for him.

"I will not do it that way," he said. "Not anymore."

He looked down at me, and I could have drowned in his eyes.

"Please." The word escaped my lips.

"I am sorry, Ms. Shaw," he said. He was kneeling next to the chaise, over me, and his head descended toward mine. I turned my face toward his, expecting another kiss, but he ducked his head lower, and his mouth found my neck instead.

I hissed as his lips touched me, the dampness of his mouth a shock against my neck that sent a wave of reaction straight down into my groin. I arched my neck, baring it to him as my hips pushed up, seeking him. His hands gripped the edges of the chaise, one on either side, barring me in. But I did not want to escape. I wanted him to touch me. My whole body ached for me to give myself to him.

I reached for him, to pull him down, but a muttered order against my skin forced me to drop my hands, and I lay helplessly burning for him as his mouth on my neck hardened, deepened.

I cried out when the pain came. Cried out—not in horror, but wanting more, needing more, an inarticulate plea as his teeth pierced my skin, slicing through it into my neck. The pain rippled out, tangled with desire, and roared over my senses, taking them to an exquisite, torturous height that demanded a release.

I could see the scarlet of the blood against the snowy white of my dress; I could feel it trickling around his lips to pool hotly beneath my shoulder. I knew what he was then, the word burning in my brain.

Vampire.

The truth of it cut through me like a knife, like his teeth at my neck. I knew now what he was, what he had wanted since I'd first walked into his office. I had my answer, more terrible than I could have imagined. And I didn't care. I couldn't care. Because all I wanted was him.

His mouth moved over my broken skin, and I could feel him suck, swallowing, taking my lifeblood into him as I wanted to take him into me. His was moving rhythmically now, each kiss a drink, and I rocked with him, panting, pleading for him to give me satisfaction.

He made a sound deep in his throat. It sent a shudder through me as I felt it against my skin. His weight came onto the edge of the chaise as he freed one arm, and he ripped away the blanket, his mouth still kissing, still torturing, still drinking. Blindly, his hand hooked around one knee and slid up my thigh. I whimpered, my hips seeking him, thighs loosening, opening myself to him.

"Oh, please," I begged, just like he'd said I would. "Please."

And then he was inside me, two fingers thrust to their limit as his thumb found my clitoris.

I came apart. The rhythm broke into a wave of heat, surging up from the root of my clitoris, tearing through my innermost core, and exploding in my brain. White lights went off behind my eyes, the rushing of blood in my ears drowning my cries, until all I could feel was him, his mouth on my neck and his fingers inside me, and the raging force that was tearing my mind to pieces. Kill me or save me, I knew I was his— completely and irrevocably his.

Then there was blood, oh God, so much blood, and my vision dimmed from blinding light as the blackness rushed up around me, stealing everything.

I fell into the darkness. His darkness.

And I was alone.

The story continues in…

BLOOD BORN

Cora's Choice – Book 2
AETHEREAL BONDS

**Want to read the first chapter right now? Sign
up for the newsletter at AetherealBonds.com
to get exclusive access—for free!
Get free content and release updates.**

Cora wakes to find herself forever changed. Mr.
Thorne's promise of healing is fulfilled, but at a terrible
price: She is now eternally bound to the immortal vampire, her mind and body forever subject to his will.

All she ever wanted was to be rid of her cancer.
But how can Cora break free from Dorian Thorne when
everything in her wants to give herself to him, and when
Dorian has sworn never to let her go?

Through her new blood-bond, Cora is thrust into a
world of great danger and strange powers. Running for
her life, she knows the only one who can save her is the
one who will never set her free.…

ABOUT THE AUTHOR

V. M. Black is the creator of Aethereal Bonds, a sensual paranormal romance urban fantasy series that takes vampires, shifters, and faes where they've never been before. You can find her on AetherealBonds.com. Visit to connect through her mailing list and various social media platforms across the web.

She's a proud geek who lives near Washington, D.C., with her family, and she loves fantasy, romance, science fiction, and historical fiction.

All of her books are available in a number of digital formats. Don't have an e-reader? No problem! You can download free reading apps made by every major retailer from your phone or tablet's app store and carry your books with you wherever you go.